I0601471

THE CAPE

Jeff Lovell

TotalRecall Publications, Inc.
1103 Middlecreek
Friendswood, Texas 77546
281-992-3131 281-482-5390 Fax
www.totalrecallpress.com

All rights reserved. Except as permitted under the United States Copyright Act of 1976, No part of this publication may be reproduced, stored in a retrieval system, or transmitted in any form or by any means electronic or mechanical or by photocopying, recording, or otherwise without prior permission of the publisher. Exclusive worldwide content publication / distribution by TotalRecall Publications, Inc.

Copyright © 2016: Jeff Lovell
Edited by: Jacqui Lovell
All rights reserved
ISBN: 978-1-59095-208-5
UPC: 6-43977-42081-7

Library of Congress Control Number: 2015951369

Printed in the United States of America with simultaneous printings in Australia, Canada, and United Kingdom.

FIRST EDITION
1 2 3 4 5 6 7 8 9 10

This is a work of fiction. The characters, names, events, views, and subject matter of this book are either the author's imagination or are used fictitiously. Any similarity or resemblance to any real people, real situations or actual events is purely coincidental and not intended to portray any person, place, or event in a false, disparaging or negative light.

The scanning, uploading and distribution of this book via the Internet or via any other means without the permission of the publisher is illegal and punishable by law. Please purchase only authorized electronic editions, and do not participate in or encourage electronic piracy of copyrighted materials. Your support of the author's rights is appreciated.

To Retha Basson, a girl from
Durban, Republic of South Africa.
Many years ago she told me the
Legend of The Flying Dutchman.

Award Winning Author

 is a native Chicagoan, with 3 degrees from the University of Illinois and an earned doctorate from Vanderbilt University. Jeff taught high school writing and literature for thirty three years and sponsored the school paper, Student Council and several other activities. He ran the drama program at two high schools, teaching and directing and designing sets, lighting and costumes. His specialty in his career focused on Shakespeare. Since he retired from education, Jeff has served as a theatre and film critic for a television station and appears frequently to review theatre and literature.

About The Book

People say that *Der Fleigen Hollander—The Flying Dutchman*, as it is known in English—vanished with all hands in the sixteenth century off the Cape of Good Hope. Yet the ship has been by reliable, truthful people all over the world, suggesting that the ship is trapped in a time warp somewhere in the treacherous ocean south of the Cape. When her father is kidnapped by the ship, Therese goes to find him and rescue him from the self-imposed, Purgatorial imprisonment. In the search she is joined by her mother and a lifetime best friend, who seek to help Therese draw his soul back from the pit of Hell before he is lost for all eternity. Or did she?

Preface

A friendless, nasty millionaire goes in search of eternal life and finds despair and violence. According to legend, he will never escape the hold of the ship, but join with the crew in living the same day over and over again for all eternity. He learns that Hell is cold: extremely cold and brutal.

Introduction

The legends say that no one escapes from the Hell Ship known as the Flying Dutchman. Yet a friendless, conniving American Millionaire finds a way to join the ghostly crew, and soon begins to lose himself in the terror of imprisonment and punishment that never ends. He learns that the price of eternal life without repentance is the loss of identity, loved ones, and personal values and any measure whatever of personal joy. When he disappears into the gloom and violence of one of the worst environments in the world, his daughter joins forces with some friends to see if they can find the legendary ship and redeem the lost soul of her father.

CHAPTER ONE

Three fishermen left the Cape Town, South Africa harbor in the early morning, heading out to fish in a small sloop. The single sail didn't propel the craft at any great speed, but it didn't matter to the men, who set out trolling lines. They talked in hushed tones as they went along. The day couldn't have been better: 60 degrees, sunny with a nice wind. Still, they were wary, knowing that the weather in the area known as the Cape of Good Hope had a bad reputation. Treacherous, their friends said. Could be dangerous.

In the late afternoon, the weather changed. Within moments they found themselves struggling against what became dangerous swells. Fishing became a secondary consideration and they began to fear for their lives. They started to turn for home as a profound fog settled in.

Then, The Ship appeared.

One man in the fishing sloop, pulling on the oars and trying to fight the swell, saw an ancient three-masted sailing vessel emerging from the mist. Bathed in a peculiar gold light, it turned toward them, sails filled with a spectral wind, gliding as if on wings. The man cried out in fear and pointed at the apparition. His two friends turned and spotted the ship moving against the wind toward them.

The three fisherman sat, staring in terror at what they beheld. None of them had never seen the golden ship, but they'd heard about it, and they knew at once what the ship was. They also knew that few people ever survived after seeing this ship.

The strange ship pulled alongside, pitching and rolling with the swells, blocking their way so they couldn't return to the port of Cape Town. Now, to their horror, they could make out the name on the prow of the ship: *Der Fliegende Hollander*. A man, also surrounded by an eerie glow, yelled down at them. The fishermen couldn't quite make out the words over the noise of the ocean, the winds and the waves. Nonetheless the fishermen knew the man was speaking Dutch, the language from which their own Afrikaans language in the city of Cape Town derived. The glowing ship came nearer, and a couple of men on the ship lowered a rope ladder.

Sometime later that night, as an all but impenetrable darkness settled in, three fishermen came home. When they entered the harbor, their minds clarified, as if they had awakened from a powerful anesthetic. They seemed to remember that they had spent the last few hours fighting for their lives in the dreadful weather off the Cape of Good Hope, and only their expert, by now instinctive, seamanship had saved them today. Somehow, they remembered that they'd managed to heave to and sprint for home, the sail on their one-master so full from the gale force winds that the small craft all but screamed across the heaving ocean. But the trip itself never quite unfolded in their minds.

The fishermen hurried into a tavern near their wharf with quite a tale to tell. A small number of the tavern patrons scoffed at the story, and a few managed to stop just short of calling the men liars. Others, grim faced and nodding, said nothing to contradict the terrifying tale of the nightmare golden ship that the fishermen related. Many of them had experienced a similar vision off the Cape. They knew what the men had seen.

The men would recover, and in a couple of weeks they would go out to fish again off the Cape. But every trip in the wild ocean off the Cape of Good Hope would clench the depths of their souls with visceral terror.

* * * * *

The ocean waters off The Cape of Good Hope, located at the southern tip of the African continent, have the reputation of being some of the worst in the world. Two great oceans intersect there: the calm, warm waters of the Indian Ocean clash with violence against the treacherous and inhospitable Atlantic. The ocean just south of the Cape of Good Hope remains cold, wild and shark infested much of the year, unwelcoming and perfidious to its name.

Many ships, some of them mighty and indestructible to all appearance, have perished in that sea over the centuries. Both sailing ships and motor powered launches have fallen victim to the storms of the Cape. Not far from the historic city of Cape Town lies a sad graveyard known as Shipwreck Beach. About 3000 vessels have come to grief along the South African coastline and many of those wrecks perished on Shipwreck Beach. Their remains stand in mute testimony to the hellish treachery of the Cape.

The name of one ship in particular tends to quiet conversation. Moreover, few ships in history have inspired more legends, more folklore and myth, many books and other writings. It has even been the subject of a famous opera by

Richard Wagner. This ship, a Dutch trading ship, left Ceylon, India, in 1659 laden with gold bullion and expensive spices. The crew of *Der Fliegende Hollander* intended to round the Cape and then hug the west coast of Africa as she made her way home to the Netherlands. *Der Fliegende Hollander* fell prey to an appalling storm off the Cape, however, and never came home. Many people believe that she went down with all hands in the freezing cold seas off of South Africa.

In all but a few cases—the legend of RMS Titanic, for example--the story of a shipwreck ends when the ship sinks. The legend of *Der Fliegende Hollander* also doesn't stop with the foundering of the ship. Indeed she remains the subject of many terrifying legends and stories. Tradition says that not only is she still out there, but she's still locked in fierce, if futile, combat with a never-ending storm off the Cape of Good Hope.

Beware, all you audacious sailors who attempt to round the Cape: the legend says you'll pay a huge price if you so much as see the ship, much less try to board her. Don't even contemplate the notion of stealing her gold. Don't flatter yourself that you can save her from her self-imposed condemnation.

On the contrary: if you should see the *Hollander*, keep going. Make full sail away from her, or push your engines to full throttle so you don't come in contact with her. *Hollander* won't chase. She can't. Her tattered sails hang from rotted crossbeams on woeful masts, her ropes and ratlines are rotting and old, and her crew, cursed for all eternity to labor in desperate fatigue, struggle against the storm every day, worn out and exhausted from four hundred some years of battle with the elements.

The members of the crew don't perceive the ship the same way as you will. They see a sea-worthy vessel, trimmed and in full sail, cutting a sharp slice through the waves at flank speed. The wind always fills her sails as they flee before an appalling storm. But they do sense that something has gone very wrong.

Tradition about *Hollander* says that her captain, named Hendrik Van Zeeland, bears much of the responsibility for his ship's plight. Fighting his way around the Cape of Good Hope on that last voyage, he went aloft and, legends say, shouted to the heavens that he would fight free of the swells and storm without the gracious and compassionate help of heaven. He yelled blasphemies and screamed imprecations—

--And the whole ship transformed. It passed from life into eternal darkness, into perpetual storm and incessant thunder and lightning, ceaseless high winds and waves in a sea famous for some of the worst weather in the world. In such conditions she remains trapped for all time.

Legends about *Hollander* persist to this day. Some of them assert that the crew knows they are cursed for everlasting. The stories claim that the condemned sailors beg and even pray for death. They would resort to any measures, any efforts, any treachery to achieve surcease of their constant struggle to sail the old rotted hulk.

Other than the skeptics, which are legion, many people say that the crew doesn't seem to realize their ship will never come home, that the very name *Der Fliegende Hollander* has become a curse, its name a synonym for lost causes that can't be abandoned.

The exotic spices from the Far East—cinnamon, nutmeg, cumin, and exotic pepper among others—no longer have any trading value, having rotted away in the ship's hold. Unlike the crew, they were not rendered imperishable. Nor can the massive amount of gold in the ship's hold purchase her freedom.

The ship sails on and on, yet never making progress, always headed northwest into the wind, despite her worthless sails being nothing more than tattered canvas. But the crew never sees the destruction, the ragged sails, or the miserable rotted timbers. To them, the ship looks as it did when they left Ceylon, blood red sails billowing, the pennants snapping in the wind. The crew still looks forward to the day when the ship at last rounds the Cape of Good Hope into the Atlantic and sails north along the coast of Africa toward home.

The sailors never get their wish, though. Every day, mountainous waves wash over the decks, near-hurricane force winds rock the ship, and the dreadful food tastes the same. Every day, the captain climbs the rigging to the top of the mainmast and screams his blasphemous curses. Every day, the ship plunges again into blackness.

* * * * *

Therese McNulty, a young American woman living and working in South Africa, studied the legend of *Der Fliegende Hollander*. She set out to discover the ship and set it free from its hell of stormy imprisonment. But she didn't covet the spices and the gold; nor did she think about rescuing the *Hollander* itself, or her tormented crewmen.

The curse of the *Hollander* had reached into her family. The crew kidnapped her father and took him aboard the ship to take the place of a crewman who learned the truth and wanted to escape the torment and imprisonment of *Hollander*.

Kidnapping the soul of another human remains the only way someone can escape from the ship known in the English speaking world as *The Flying Dutchman*.

CHAPTER TWO

avid M. "Mac" McNulty enjoyed the somewhat sinister reputation he'd cultivated over the years. Many of those who had dealings with him referred to him—though not to his face—as "Graybeard."

To be sure, no one intended that the name should be considered by any means complimentary, because it depicted him as a pirate. Indeed few nicknames ever fit a person better. With dashing mutton-chop sideburns, long hair and anachronistic clothing, he lacked only an eye-patch and a cutlass to appear as a pirate.

The depiction of him as a swashbuckler fit like a surgical glove. He launched raids on companies, and his hostile takeovers cost many people their jobs. He would bleed the companies, steal away assets, sell properties and equipment, hide money and then abandon the lifeless shell of the company. People would characterize him as ruthless, unprincipled, and friendless.

But he also had staggering riches.

Mac had shown extraordinary skill in training at Wall Street, going out on his own as a commodities trader. Mac loved the game of hard rock business, which almost always involved screwing over everyone who got in his way. Women found him attractive because of his almost sinister good looks, his bitter sense of humor, and his money. Mostly his money.

Mac had been married a few times, though he gave up on making his relationships in any sense permanent. He tired with some rapidity of the women who shared his bed, which he placed in a room decorated with mirrors, with silks and with erotic paintings. He lived convinced that he could find the woman whose sexual abilities would transform him, who would overwhelm him with pleasure night after night and who took her greatest joy in life in making sure he was gratified.

For the most part, the women he dumped left the relationship angry at him, yet a few felt sorry for him. To know that he had their sympathy would have astounded him, to be sure. He regarded himself as the one getting rid of a non-gratifying partner. He grew more and more bitter with each discarded woman that he perceived to have failed in meeting his preposterous expectations and fantasies.

His non-fulfilling experience resulted, of course, in a general hatred of women, despite the physical attraction he felt for them. He didn't care that they were accomplished, articulate, intelligent or well-educated. He didn't care about children though he had several. He often couldn't remember the names of his offspring. He often couldn't remember how many he had.

He spent a fair amount of money bailing his children out of jail and getting them out of trouble at schools. He liked to blame the teachers who worked with them. Those teachers, he sneered. He knew the truth, he scoffed. See, they didn't understand or like his kids. The teachers were jealous of him—yeah, that was it--because the teachers had no money but they knew that Mac had all he could ever spend in several lifetimes.

Mac did not transact his piracy with a cutlass, a Jolly Roger waving on a flagpole on his quarterdeck, wearing an eyepatch or a pegleg. Nor did his pirating involve murder, in the direct sense of the word, but many of his victims fell into poor health and died after he destroyed them. Nor did it involve cannons, though his business methods did as much damage as Blackbeard's cannon broadsides at a helpless ship.

His piracy consisted of hostility to other people and organizations. Mac loved the thrill of the hunt, the terror he inspired, the defeated expressions on the face of his victims as they saw him loot and destroy businesses they'd worked for years to build up and nurture and make into things of beauty, growing in the flinty soil of competitive business to become profitable, reliable, well thought of and significant in their contributions to society.

When Mac reached his lifetime financial goal, he at last felt safe. Almost at the same moment, though, his doctors told him that he had all but destroyed his health. His insides had been wrecked: duodenal ulcers, a weak heart, and less than terrific kidneys. So, he bought a yacht and christened it *Arcturus*, the name of the brightest star on the northern half of Earth's sky dome. He hired a crew and a superb chef, stocked his yacht with expensive food and liquor and set off to see the world. He headed west from San Francisco across the Pacific, visiting the great countries of China, Japan, and the Southeast Asian countries. From there he made his way to India, and then down the east coast of Africa.

His yacht reached the Cape of Good Hope, the extreme southern tip of the African Continent, in the midst of a gale, a dreadful night for sailing. His captain suggested they make for shelter on the mainland and wait out the gale, but to his captain's surprise, Mac sneered at the suggestion. He directed the captain to take *Arcturus* into some of the worst seas in the world.

Mac, grasping handholds and staggering, came onto the bridge at 12:30 A.M. to demand an explanation for his discomfort brought on by the high seas and uncomfortable conditions of the Cape of Good Hope. The captain, Steve Blair, saw him coming and sighed to himself. Mac's appearance meant a humiliating dressing down in front of the bridge crew.

"What's going on, Blair?" demanded Mac McNulty. "We're being jolted out of bed down there."

"Rough night, Sir," returned Blair. "Forty, fifty foot swells, driving rain, lightning—not a great time to round the Horn. I suggest we back out and wait this one out."

"Are we in danger?" said McNulty.

"Well, bigger ships than ours *have* gone down in this region, Sir."

McNulty waved his hand in some impatience. He did not like enigmatic answers. He most liked answers that supported his preconceived notions, and, given his wealth and intimidating personality, few people could overcome his formidable character. "Don't give me that," he snarled. "When I ask you a question, I want a direct answer."

"I gave it, sir," said Steve. "She's a fine ship and she will do as well as any could in these seas."

"So?" demanded McNulty.

"So, I consider this situation dangerous, sir," said Steve, forcing himself to stay calm but enjoying a mental picture of the owner lying flat on his back, massaging his aching jaw, his nose flattened and bleeding, while his captain stood over him rubbing his knuckles. "The South African National Weather Service calls this one of the worst storms in years, and they say it'll blow for several days. Again: please let me recommend that we return to Durban for a week and come back again, or make for Cape Town Harbor. We are in desperate danger."

"Are you guaranteeing safe passage after that week?" persisted McNulty.

"Of course I can't do that, sir," said Steve. "But…"

"Take us through, then," said McNulty. "A few hours and we'll round the Cape, right?"

"I hope so, Sir," said Steve. "But I can't guarantee that either."

"Are you afraid?" demanded McNulty.

"Yes, Sir, I sure am," asserted Steve. "A storm on the Cape is never trivial, and this one looks like a classic."

"Take us through," said McNulty with an imperious wave, making clear his disgust at what he considered his captain's poltroonery.

Steve nodded, said "Aye, sir." *Is he trying to commit suicide*? Steve asked himself, not for the first time. McNulty had been taking elaborate and unnecessary risks the whole voyage.

The owner's opinion notwithstanding, Steve's instincts about the danger were correct. McNulty's order would prove to be an unwise decision, to say the least.

McNulty turned to leave the bridge, but a swell smacked the side of the yacht, knocking him off balance. He gripped the navigation console, cursing and snarling his displeasure.

Steve turned back to the navigation, shaking his head in dismay. This incident had pretty well confirmed his unspoken decision to leave McNulty's employ, and he knew that most of the crew had had enough, also. He glanced at his radar, did a double take, and then stared in surprise at what he saw. In the next few moments, everything would change.

CHAPTER THREE

McKenna Byrne descended from the Lufthansa jet at King Shaka International Airport in Durban, South Africa. Her husband Clint would join her the next day, but several business deals had forced him to remain in their hometown in Northern Illinois. In the meantime, she intended to spend time catching up with her college roommate, Therese McNulty. Therese had called McKenna and asked her friend for help in trying to figure out what had happened to her Father, Mac McNulty.

McKenna and her husband Clint had been part of a couple of treasure hunting teams the last few years. Together, they'd found the lost horde of Sir Henry Morgan on a remote desert island in the Virgin Islands. McKenna had been part of a couple of other teams. One had uncovered the treasure of Sandy Gordon in New Hampshire, and another group that had discovered the treasure of Edward Teach in North Carolina.

The young couple had become wealthy, and had decided to use some of the treasure to help sponsor their advanced education plans. Both of them had graduated with doctorates from prestigious programs at major universities.

McKenna shifted her thoughts to the phone call she'd received a few days ago. She had been cleaning the lovely house that she and her husband Clint had purchased in St. Charles,

Illinois, located near the Fox River in the western suburbs of Chicago. The phone rang and saw to her surprise that the call originated from the Republic of South Africa.

She flipped open her phone and grinned as her best friend, Therese McNulty, greeted her. McKenna hadn't laid eyes on her friend since Therese had been part of McKenna's wedding party three years earlier. They'd written letters and continued their friendship with the internet and satellite phones, but McKenna's job as a high school teacher and her work on the doctorate at the University of Illinois, as well as her marriage to Clint, had precluded her ability to get away for a visit.

"Therese, what a surprise," she grinned. "How are you?"

"Oh, I'm okay, Mickey, but I could really use your help."

"Me?" said McKenna.

"Well, Clint too, if you can manage it," said Therese.

"Sure, we don't have anything in particular going on," said McKenna. "When are you coming in?"

"No, that's not it," said Therese. "I want you guys to come here."

"To South Africa?" gasped McKenna. "Are you kidding?"

"No, I'm as serious as a nuclear attack, Mick," returned her friend. "Look, I'll make all the arrangements, pay for your tickets, and so on—"

"Therese, has something happened?" asked McKenna. "You wouldn't be getting married, would you?"

"No, no," said her friend. "This is much more serious."

"More serious than a marriage?" chuckled McKenna.

"Please, Mickey," pleaded her friend. "I need your specific skills, you and Clint, here in Cape Town. We'll be going to sea off of The Cape of Good Hope, to be exact."

McKenna found herself now bewildered at her former college roommate's request. "Can you tell me about it?"

"I'd rather do it when you arrive, okay?" said her friend. "I really can't explain on the phone. But please trust me, it's vital that you come."

"Well, okay, I think," said McKenna. "I'll e-mail you the arrangements. Can you give me a hint what's going on?"

Therese hesitated. "Okay," she said at last. "Read up on the Legend of the Flying Dutchman."

Flabbergasted, McKenna stammered an okay, and she and her friend rang off.

McKenna had said goodbye to her friend and began to make the arrangements to go to the Republic of South Africa. She visited the library and checked some information on the mysterious ship known as *The Flying Dutchman*.

That evening Clint listened to his wife and agreed with the plans, excited to see the beautiful country at the southernmost tip of the African Continent. He liked Therese a great deal and knew how much his wife loved her friend.

McKenna thought about how they'd pursued their advanced degrees: Clint had worked on a Doctorate in Clinical Psychology, and McKenna completed her doctorate in Early Childhood Psychology. Both husband and wife never shrank from challenges, and had supported one another through the pain, the drudgery and the heartache of pursuing the degrees.

McKenna cherished one memory of her husband coming into their bedroom, finding her lying on the floor, weeping with frustration as she struggled to make sense of her dissertation topic. His kindness and his gentle embrace drove away the pain of the frustration. He sat with her on the floor and talked with her for two hours about her work. Then they sat at the kitchen table together for four hours the next day, making notes on a legal pad, and she just talked about what she'd been discovering in her research, writing on her outline and her drafts, answering his questions, working with her husband to understand some difficult concepts.

At the end of that conference, McKenna had an outline of the paper in her hand. She knew where the paper was headed, what she needed to do, how to apply the data, and most important, they'd worked out a tentative thesis statement. She saw now what she needed to say, how to organize it, and how she could pull the whole paper together.

When they finished, he hugged her and told her how proud he was of her. She finished the dissertation in six weeks and defended the paper before her doctoral committee at Gregory Hall, on the south end of the Quad at the University of Illinois two weeks after that.

McKenna had gained a great deal of academic knowledge in writing her dissertation, to be sure. However, the most important thing to her would always be the realization of how much her husband loved her, how much pride he took in her, and how much he valued who she was.

She knew, also, that their intimacy had changed. Though it had never been unsatisfying in any sense, McKenna began to see their sexual relationship as an opportunity for her to pay him back for the love he had for her, and to express the love she felt for him. Their whole relationship matured and strengthened.

McKenna regarded her dissertation as the most difficult and demanding undertaking of her life. She had gained a great deal from her Ph. D. program: not only in terms of knowledge, but also in diligence, self-confidence, and other personal qualities. The best part of her program, she understood, came in realizing how much her husband loved, valued, respected and esteemed her.

But when she and Clint had concluded their doctoral programs, finishing their degrees within a few weeks of each other, they decided to take some time and travel to exotic places, to see beauties and wonders and paintings and sculptures and mountains.

She and Clint sat at the top of Mount Haleakala in Maui and watched the sunrise, teeth chattering at the mountaintop cold but stunned with the beauty of the Hawaiian dawn. They ate fresh boiled lobster and blueberry cake at a picnic table, watching huge waves break and soar at the Pemaquid Point Lighthouse in southeast Maine. They played golf in San Antonio, Texas, after touring the Alamo and studying the history of the historic conflict. They toured the aquarium in Monterey, California, and enjoyed the sea otters, a species once believed hunted to extinction but now making a remarkable comeback. They hiked through the Valley of the Yellowstone River, staggered by the majesty of the waterfalls, woods, and mountains of America's premier national park.

* * * * *

McKenna walked across the Tarmac looking for her friend Therese, but still thinking about her husband. She and Clint hadn't spent many nights apart since their marriage and her bed felt empty and forlorn when he wasn't snuggled to her. She wouldn't tell just anyone, of course, but she would tell her best friend Therese...

Where the heck was she? thought McKenna.

McKenna sighed again, and smiled to think about Clint. Few people knew that he had a unique ability inherited from the ancient race known as Faerae, whose abilities terrified the early inhabitants of England. One of them, Myrthynne, had been a chief advisor to the legendary King Arthur because of his ability, called the *Cymreig*, to see what others were thinking.

McKenna entered the terminal and walked toward an information kiosk. She didn't notice that she received more than a few delighted stares from fellow passengers and airline employees. They saw the striking blaze of red hair that McKenna had inherited from her beautiful Mother, Anna O'Neill Fixx, and they observed her graceful figure and striking height. McKenna, who stood almost six feet tall, also had vivid blue eyes and a beautiful Irish complexion.

In particular an older woman and two gigantic men focused on McKenna. Their stares were not as much based in McKenna's attractiveness as in making sure that she was the young woman they'd been sent to apprehend. They compared a photograph to McKenna, nodded to one another and set off to follow her at a discreet distance until they could find a place to capture her with as little disturbance as possible.

McKenna's mother, Anna O'Neill, like Clint a descendant of the ancient magical race of Faerae, had worked with Clint for the last few years to help him deal with the Cymreig, the ability that had always made him something of an outcast. Before working with Anna, he would often terrify people with his ability. So he tried never to use it until his mother-in-law taught him ways to control it.

Anna's warm, gracious help, combined with the transformative love McKenna showed Clint, had given him new confidence. He had gained a deeper acceptance of himself and his abilities. He learned not to be ashamed of what he could do, but to embrace it and use it to benefit others.

McKenna's smile widened as she thought about the wonderful things he'd learned to do for others, to help them with self-confidence, personal assurance and self-worth.

McKenna and Clint felt that within a year they wanted to start a family. She told him that she felt a lack in her life because she was an only child, and she'd always wished she had brothers and sisters. Furthermore, she wanted a dozen children, perhaps six males. "Is that negotiable?" asked her husband, with a serious expression on his face.

"Maybe," she said. "But your concessions will be significant."

He groaned and she laughed.

McKenna, still oblivious to the three people trailing her, kept scanning the crowd at the Durban airport for her friend, Therese McNulty. Her invitation to McKenna and Clint to join her in the resort city had seemed enigmatic in its obscurity, but McKenna felt thrilled at the prospect of visiting South Africa. She couldn't wait to tour the Kruger Game Reserve, to see Table Rock in Cape Town, the diamond mines in Johannesburg, and all the other fabulous attractions of the beautiful country. She and Clint had learned to surf in Hawaii and she almost danced in her eagerness to go to Jeffreys Bay. J Bay, which had been made famous in Bruce Brown's films *The Endless Summer* and *The Endless Summer II*, lay about an hour's drive southeast of Port Elizabeth.

Still no sign of Therese. Oh well, sighed McKenna. She often thought that her roommate would show up late to a serious cancer operation. She pulled out her satellite phone and called her husband.

It took a few moments to make the connection, but at last Clint came on the line. "Yeah?" he grumbled. "Whaddya want?"

She giggled. "I want to know where you are," she said. "I'm on the ground in Durban, but no Therese."

"Am I to understand that you find yourself surprised by that?" he asked. "Not finding Therese, I mean, not being on the ground."

"No, I can't say I'm surprised," she said. "But I really don't know what to do now. I don't have a phone number for her. I thought she'd be here."

"Well, maybe she's held up in traffic?" he said, trying to comfort his wife on the other side of the world.

"I suppose," sighed McKenna.

"I'm about to board the plane and take off from O'Hare," he said. "The limo dropped me about an hour ago. Then, it's about 24 hours of flying, as you know so well. So if you want to wait there…"

"I don't," she groaned.

"I reiterate my previous question," her husband said. "Why South Africa? Why now?"

"What's the temp there now?" she asked.

"Huh," he said. "Probably single digits, with snow and fifty mile per hour winds."

"Right," she said. "It's 80 degrees here, with blue skies, a gentle breeze and an almost overpowering scent of flowers."

"Oh," he said. "In that case I withdraw the question."

"We can surf as soon as you get here, I think," she said. "I'm in beautiful weather."

A woman approached her and spoke in Afrikaans, one of the youngest official languages on the planet, very much related to Dutch. McKenna put a finger up, closed off with her husband and folded her phone. "Yes?" she smiled.

"Mrs. Byrne?" said the woman.

"Yes," nodded McKenna.

"Let me introduce myself," said the woman, switching with ease into English. McKenna smiled, knowing that a great many South Africans are as fluent in English as in Afrikaans. Her accent sounded British, reflecting one of the two major influences in the settlers who had come to the country, the Dutch and the British. "My name is Retha Basson. Miss McNulty sent me to bring you to her."

"I see," said McKenna. "I'm sure you understand that for me to go off with a perfect stranger is, of course, completely out of the question."

"Quite right, quite right," said the woman. She appeared to be perhaps 60 years old, with a brilliant smile and a disarming sweetness about her. "However, I do have some credentials." Miss Basson handed McKenna a business card, then a driver's license, and then a sealed envelope. McKenna turned the envelop over and found, as was her roommate's custom, sealing wax on the flap with Therese's stamp that McKenna recognized at once.

She opened the envelope and found that her friend had written the letter.

"McKenna," it read. "I apologize that I have to have my friend Retha meet you. Please understand that I have known her for years and trust her. Also please let her bring you to me. Something terribly significant has happened. Love, Therese."

"I don't doubt that it is legitimate," said McKenna. "But my husband plans to meet me here tomorrow, and I have no way of reaching him now. He's in the airplane as we speak. I really can't go anywhere until he arrives--"

The woman interrupted and her tone changed. "Mrs. Byrne," she said. "I'm afraid you don't understand. You *are* coming with us." She opened her purse and removed a small pistol which she pointed at McKenna.

Chapter Four

Now McKenna became aware that two large men had come to stand just behind her. She turned and saw that they had their hands thrust into their pockets. "I see," she said. Oh, boy, she said to herself. She took a deep breath, let out half of it and fell into her training she and Clint received at a karate school in Champaign while they'd been working on their doctorates at the University of Illinois. McKenna lashed out like a cobra and broke the woman's wrist with a powerful whip kick. The gun skidded across the ground and the woman screamed as the pain of a compound fracture hit with excruciating full force.

She turned to the man on her left and hit him in the throat with the knuckles of her right hand. He doubled over with pain and McKenna, in almost the same motion, kicked the man to her right behind his left knee. The knee buckled and he started to crumble, but before he could shout with the pain, she launched a kick that snapped his head back. The whole fight had taken about five seconds.

McKenna saw the airport security running toward the scene, but she didn't stop. The second man was trying to regain his balance and she gave him a shot to the throat that left him gasping for breath. The first man, still choking, tried to say something but she kicked him hard in the knee, crumpling him to the ground.

"All right," yelled an airport security man. "It's over." McKenna dropped into a defensive stance and backed away out of the triangle of people she'd just demolished. She put her hands up in surrender to the Airport security.

"I'm unarmed," she said. "I'm an American citizen. These people were attempting to abduct me." One of the Airport men came to stand next to her. A woman in a uniform came over and did a cursory search of McKenna while other security men came running up. They twisted plastic ties onto the men's wrists, but pinioned the woman.

A few minutes later, The Durban police arrived took the three people into custody. A detective named Kenney stood with McKenna.

"Mrs. Byrne," he said. "I apologize for your rude introduction to our country. Do you know what they wanted with you?"

"I'm here to visit my friend and college roommate," said McKenna. "The woman gave me a letter from her. I don't know what to make of it now." She showed Kenney the letter. "My friend wrote this."

He looked over the letter. "McNulty?"

"Yes," she nodded. "We lived together when we went to college in the United States, she served at my wedding and we've remained best friends. She wrote to me and we've been e-mailing back and forth. I'm suspicious that she never contacted me about having someone meet me, but that letter sure looks like her handwriting."

"Why did you use force?" he asked.

"They threatened me," she said. "The woman pulled a gun.

That one, yes," she said, pointing to a twenty-two caliber pistol that another agent held up.

"It might be wise for you to leave the country," said Kenney.

McKenna nodded. "I would," she said. "But my husband is supposed to meet me here in about 24 hours. He just boarded the plane to come here and as I'm sure you know, the trip from the U.S. is a long and difficult one."

"Where had you planned to stay?" he asked.

"I have a reservation at the Hilton," she said. "The guide books say it's about thirteen miles from the airport, is that right?"

"Yes," said the man. "I wonder if you could please come with us to the police station? We'll be happy to take you anywhere you wish, but we would like to book the men and the woman. They may need to be hospitalized."

"I take no pleasure in hurting them, Sir," said McKenna. "I perceived that I had to defend myself."

"Quite right, quite right," he assented with some haste. "But we would like to interview you about the event."

"Am I under arrest?" asked McKenna. At this point, she wanted to get on a flight and return home. But she couldn't let her husband arrive and not know what had happened.

"Certainly not," he said. "We're merely asking for your help."

"I guess I can stay one day," she told Kenney. So, with some reluctance, she nodded assent and accompanied the man to the waiting car.

To her surprise, a great many of the airline employees and passengers had lined up on either side of the exit. They began to applaud when she came into view and reached out to shake her hand. McKenna, red-faced with embarrassment, touched many of the hands and smiled as she heard the flash of many cameras. Reporters asked her to comment for the local papers, and she promised she'd talk to them after she met with the police.

At the police station, an officer led her into a room with a two way mirror. On the other side of the glass she saw the three people who had intimidated her. She identified them and noted with a little secret satisfaction that they looked a lot worse than she felt.

A policewoman showed her into a comfortable waiting room and gave her coffee, water and a sandwich. She looked at a magazine, but found that it was written in Afrikaans and gave up. She said to the matron in the room, "I would really like to leave, please."

"Yes, yes," said the woman. "A few moments, please."

An hour went by, and McKenna's annoyance turned to anger. When at last the door opened and a man entered, she stood, aware that smoke might have been coming out of her ears.

"Mrs. Byrne," he said, and she heard the Afrikaans twang in his voice.

"Yes," she said. "Forgive me, but I don't speak Afrikaans."

He waved the apology aside. "It is no matter," he said. "I wonder if we can talk for a few moments."

"Are you a policeman?" she asked. He hesitated and she said, "In that case, please open the door and let me leave. I have nothing to say that I have not already said."

A large smile appeared on his face. "Would you like a job?" he asked.

"A job," she said, dumbfounded.

"My name is Holbart," he said. "I am the head of South African security and I just came over from Praetoria. We would be very glad to have you on our side," he concluded, and showed her his credentials.

"What do you mean?" she asked.

"Mrs. Byrne, you just beat up three of my agents," he said.

"What?" she gasped.

"Yes," he said. "They believed that they were apprehending a criminal. I didn't brief them properly, I'm afraid, and you did what I would have expected, given your skills and international reputation."

"I have an international reputation?" she said.

"Oh yes," he said. "You found the treasures of Blackbeard, of Sandy Gordon, and the lost horde of Sir Henry Morgan, is that not true?"

"Well, yes," she said. "At least, I served as part of the teams that found them."

"You also have a name for being quick witted and exceptional in your hand to hand combat skills."

"Thank you," she said. "That's very flattering and kind."

"So?" he grinned. "Could we persuade you and your husband to move to our beautiful country?"

"Thank you, no," she said. "I believe you when you say that you consider The Republic of South Africa a beautiful country. However all I've seen of your country is this police station and the airport."

"I know," he said. "We will make it up to you."

"Why do you care about me?" she asked.

"Your good friend, Therese McNulty, contacted us," he said. "Her father has gone missing at sea."

McKenna stared. "Mac McNulty has vanished?"

"Yes," he said. "She has been busy for the last several days trying to bring the situation under control. She apologizes for not meeting you, and said she will explain when she sees you. The story could well become part of the Lore of South Africa, unfortunately."

"What do you mean?"

He didn't answer at once. "Mrs. Byrne," he said. "Will you please be my guest this evening rather than going to the hotel?"

"What?" she said.

"Yes," he said. "My wife and I would be honored to have you to come to our home in Pretoria for dinner and night's sleep. I will have my men meet your husband in the morning and bring him to us."

"Whatever my international reputation," she smiled, "I certainly couldn't be shrewish enough to say n0to such a generous offer." He laughed.

CHAPTER FIVE

A few moments later, McKenna stepped off the elevator at the heliport at the top of the Durban Police station and boarded the Minister's private helicopter to the Durban airport. The trip was 540 kilometers, he told her, but that would enable him to show her a little of the country. The Minister had his men cancel her reservations, collect her luggage and contact her husband en route to the airport.

McKenna's first helicopter ride thrilled her, and the Minister's private plane was lovely and gracious. The Minister had his pilot head a little north and east of Pretoria. They swooped over the Kruger game reserve so he could show her some of the wildlife in the reserve. At one point he indicated a herd of elephants.

"They can be a problem despite their intelligence," he said.

"In what sense? Do you mean because of their size?" she asked.

"They have a weakness for plums," he laughed.

McKenna, mystified, asked: "You mean, the fruit plums?"

"Yes," he said. "They eat the plums whole, and they do not digest them well. So, when the fruit sits in their stomachs, rather than being digested, it ferments."

"You mean, turns to alcohol," she smiled.

"Do you see?" he asked.

"So you can have a herd of drunken elephants?"

"Alas," he said.

She began to laugh. "I'm sorry," she apologized. "But the picture of a drunken elephant…"

He smiled and directed the pilot to go to his home. McKenna changed into a formal outfit and the Minister's driver took them to a beautiful five star restaurant called La Madeleine.

The owner, Daniel Leusch and his wife Karine greeted the Minister. "We first opened the restaurant more than thirty years ago," Daniel told McKenna, as she took his arm to walk to their table. "We like the tranquility of Lynnwood Ridge."

"What does the restaurant's name mean?" asked McKenna.

"Ah," said Karine, holding the chair for the minister's wife. "The name comes from the shell shaped Madeleine biscuit."

"Marcel Proust once wrote that it 'invades the senses with exquisite pleasure'," said her husband.

"The same may be said of this restaurant," agreed the Minister, and Daniel and Karine smiled their thanks.

The restaurant and its delicious fare almost overwhelmed McKenna. Though she had eaten in some fine restaurants, she found this place elegant and delightful. The décor, soft and tasteful, was exceeded only by the marvelous cuisine.

They returned to the Minister's residence a few hours later. "Mrs. Byrne," said her host. "I must tell you. I think another house guest will greet us."

"Yes?" smiled McKenna.

He nodded, but didn't smile or offer any further information. Again, the enigmatic statement puzzled her, as had a great deal in The Republic of South Africa.

At the house, a smiling butler opened the door for her and

the Minister's wife showed her to a private bedroom. She went into the attached washroom, took a shower and changed into her pajamas.

When she came out, she found Therese McNulty sitting across the room in a large wing chair.

CHAPTER SIX

McKenna almost choked with surprise. "Good Grief, Therese," she managed. "Where did you come from?"

"Nice to see you, too," said her friend, making a nice effort at a smile while she rose and crossed to McKenna. The two friends hugged in greeting, but McKenna could feel the tension in her friend's body. "The Minister brought me up here from Cape Town. I'm sorry I didn't meet you at the airport, but I did ask the Secret Service guys to pick you up. I'm really sorry about what happened at the airport. I mean that you found yourself in a fistfight in your first few moments in the country. That would not be typical, please believe me."

"Therese, what on earth did…"

"When does Clint get here?" interrupted her friend.

"Tomorrow, about 10:00 A. M. local time," said McKenna. "Why?"

Her friend hesitated. "Let me answer that later," she said. "First let me tell you what has happened."

McKenna shrugged. "Okay," she said.

"My dad went missing at sea," said Therese. "He vanished off his yacht as he tried to round the Cape of Good Hope."

"Vanished?" gasped McKenna. "He fell overboard?"

"His crew says they don't know what happened," nodded Therese. "But the problem goes deeper. A man in a Cape Town hospital looks just like him, talks with his voice, and so forth, but Mickey, I swear he isn't my dad."

McKenna sat with her mouth agape, staring at her friend. "What on earth does *that* mean?"

"The man in the hospital isn't my dad," asserted her friend. "So I contacted you and Clint and asked you to come."

"Therese," began McKenna. "This sounds crazy. What can we do?"

"You've told me many times about your encounters with the occult," said Therese. "Ghosts, earthbound spirits and like that."

"I guess I have," said McKenna. "But I don't *know* anything about the occult. The people with me—my father Casey, my uncle McClelland Logan, a few others—knew what to do, I didn't."

"Please, Mickey," said her friend. "I don't know whom else to turn to." Now McKenna's best friend began to cry. McKenna couldn't remember the last time she'd seen her friend that upset and scared.

No, not scared, she realized. *Terrified.*

CHAPTER SEVEN

McKenna, still recovering from finding her old friend in her room, hugged Therese again and asked her to sit on the bed with her.

"I didn't think you had much of a relationship with your father," McKenna said to her friend, as Therese applied a handkerchief to her eyes.

"He seems to be a man almost incapable of love, I know," shrugged Therese. "No, he never showed a lot of interest in me until he hired me to work down here in Cape Town."

"For the company here in South Africa?"

"Well, yes," said Therese. "I seem to have inherited his business sense, if not his ruthless nature. I'm in charge of the division of the company that manages the hospitality entities—the hotels, the restaurants, and the like—here in South Africa. I don't mean to brag, but we do pretty well. I've got very good people working for me, and my job isn't as difficult as you might think."

"Have you grown closer with your father?" asked McKenna. "Since you've been working here, I mean?

"I don't know about closer," shrugged Therese. "He seems to trust me, and pretty much leaves me alone. He remains at odds with my mother, of course."

"Does he still send her support?" asked McKenna.

"Yes, he takes very good care of her," nodded her friend, and McKenna raised an eyebrow. "But she and he don't always get along. It's very hard, even at our age, to find yourself poised between your parents, to be asked to take sides in disagreements and disputes."

McKenna now became aware of intense fatigue. "I'm jet lagged," she said. "Let's get after this in the morning, can we?"

Her friend nodded. "Of course," she said. "Mickey. Would you mind if I sleep in here with you?"

McKenna blinked. The oversized bed seemed about the size of a king-sized bed in America. "Sure, of course I don't mind," she said. "But don't you have a room?"

"Yes, I do," said Therese. "But I'm so scared I don't want to be alone."

"Scared?" said McKenna, feeling a chill spread over her.

"Yes," said Therese. "I haven't told you everything. I'm terrified."

Again a deep chill spread through McKenna's system. "Okay," she said. "We'll talk when Clint gets here."

As tired as she was, McKenna had a hard time falling asleep. The quiet of the room haunted her. When she did sleep, her dreams scared her.

Therese wouldn't scare over nothing at all. McKenna had always considered her roommate all but fearless. What could frighten her this much?

CHAPTER EIGHT

cKenna didn't awake until almost eleven in the morning. When she finally did stir, Therese had left the room. Across the room, a tray with orange juice, a carafe of coffee and an assortment of rolls stood on a table.

McKenna rose, put on a robe and crossed to the table. She took the tray and carried it out through the double doors onto a balcony where she sat to enjoy the breakfast that had been provided. She found the juice cold and refreshing, the coffee hot and stimulating. *I wouldn't mind staying here the whole trip*, she grinned to herself. She read the newspaper folded next to the tray and let herself enjoy the beautiful bedroom, the balcony and the view of Pretoria.

A light tap on the door behind her made her turn her head. Therese came out onto the balcony and poured herself some coffee.

"What time does Clint get here?" she asked.

McKenna glanced at her watch. "I forgot to reset it," she said, and adjusted it to local time. "I think he'll land in an hour or so."

"Okay," said her friend. "The Minister is going to take us down to Cape Town. He said his men will bring Clint there, okay?"

"Sure," said McKenna. "Does Clint know what's going on?"

"The Minister has talked to him on the phone when he landed," said her friend, reaching for a piece of melon. "I'm sure the Minister has everything under control."

Two hours later, the Minister's private plane lifted off, bound for the Cape Town International Airport.

"Therese," said McKenna. "How did you become so close to the Minister and his family? Why do they treat you, and even me, as if we were royalty?"

"It's because of my father," said Therese. "He has extensive holdings here in this country, and that includes diamonds, gold, and oil, which is just now coming into prominence."

"Didn't you used to tell me that his people were afraid of him?" McKenna asked. "I've always held the impression that he's never been especially well-liked anywhere he went."

"Yes," said Therese. "And that includes me. He's always been a nasty, scary man."

"How'd he persuade those women to marry him?" asked McKenna. "I thought he's had at least a couple of wives."

"Yes," nodded her friend. "That includes my mother, his first wife."

"Oh, I haven't even asked how she's doing," McKenna apologized.

"She lives in New York, as always," shrugged Therese, "and she's in great health. But Dad broke her heart when he divorced her, as you can imagine."

"How does she feel about him now?"

"It's complicated," said Therese. "I think they still love one another, but she hates him at the same time."

"Love Hate relationship," nodded McKenna.

"I called her when he went missing," Therese shrugged.

"She's on the way here also. Maybe caught the same airplanes as Clint."

McKenna was puzzled. "Why?"

"As I say, it's difficult, to say the least," said Therese. "He always goes back to her for advice, for nurture, the things that husbands do with wives. Though I don't think sex becomes involved, nor has it been since they divorced."

"I'm sorry," said McKenna. "I just don't get how a relationship like that can work."

Therese remained silent for a few moments. Then, "She still loves him. They got married when they'd just finished college, and she became pregnant with me in a couple of months."

"Oh," said McKenna. "I shouldn't have pried to such private stuff, Therese."

Therese waved the apology aside. "Mom grew up as a quiet Catholic girl, twelve years of parochial schools, three years of college, and then she transferred to the school my dad attended. She fell in love with him, graduated, had me, and settled in while he went to work. He started on this entrepreneurial stuff and made a fortune. He divorced her and married someone else."

McKenna listened to the drone of the aircraft. A hostess brought them each a ginger ale. "But you stayed loyal to him," she said.

"Yeah, I guess so," said Therese. "I think it was the case of a little girl scared to death of being alone. I remember I went for months thinking they got divorced because of me. I thought that if I was very, very good and didn't misbehave Daddy would come back. Or at least Mommy wouldn't leave too."

"Oh, Therese," began McKenna.

"After a while I got used to seeing Daddy just on occasion, and infrequent occasions at that," continued her friend. "He never came to graduations, or saw me off to proms, or anything like that. When I graduated with my MBA, he sent me a check and a ticket to Johannesburg. Yes, a few months after your wedding."

"Right, I remember you telling me you were going," said McKenna.

"I came here and went to work for one of his companies, in the equivalent of the mailroom," said Therese. "Within two years they put me in charge of the place."

"I suppose you had to deal with nepotism charges," said McKenna.

"Some at first, but when I assumed control the company took off," said Therese. "I cleared out some dead wood, like workers who'd retired on the job, brought in some new people, and now we've become one of the most productive of the companies in the McNulty family."

"Neat," smiled McKenna.

Therese shrugged. "I love what I do, and I have fun doing it," she said. "You wouldn't call it much for the social aspect, as you can imagine—"

"We're talking workaholism?" said McKenna.

"To some extent," agreed her friend. "But I work hard to make sure the people who report to me put in a reasonable day, take time off, take vacations, all that. I mean, it's okay for me to work long hours since I don't have a family or even a steady boyfriend, but I know that people who work too much become counter-productive. So I work hard, but then when I have time off I play hard, with surfing, or golf, or sailing."

"But no—ah--romance?"

"I see a couple of people, have dinner, go to movies, like that," said her friend. "But in general I'm pretty dull."

The plane began its descent into Cape Town airspace and landed within ten minutes. "Leave your bags," Therese told her. "The guys will take them to our hotel."

A limousine waited on the tarmac for Therese and the two women climbed in. "Take us to Groote Schuur Hospital," Therese told the driver.

"The hospital?" asked McKenna. Therese nodded.

"I'll explain when we get there," she said. "And I think your hubby will meet us there." Therese spent some time pointing out the sites of Cape Town as they went, about a 15 minute drive from the airport. They entered at the main entrance and went into a large reception area.

"Hey," said Clint Byrne, crossing the main lobby and embracing his wife. McKenna re-introduced her friend to her husband and they chatted for a few moments.

"Yeah, someone contacted me on the plane from the Minister's office," said Clint. "They put me on another plane and shipped me over here, but I don't have a clue what's going on."

McKenna nodded. "Therese and I will explain," she said.

"Clint," said Therese. "I know it's a secret, but you do have the Cymreig, right?"

"Well, yes," admitted Clint. "I don't use it very often, but…"

"We need your help," said Therese. "Would you come with me?"

"Sure," he said, with a glance at his wife. McKenna shrugged, as if to say, 'I don't have a clue either.'

They were shown to a private room in the non-secure psychiatric ward at one end of the massive hospital complex. McKenna took Clint's arm and attempted to fill him in on some of the story of Mac McNulty's attempt to round the Cape of Good Hope as they walked.

They entered a room with the shades drawn and dim illumination from a small night light. An old man lay on the bed, not moving, staring at the ceiling. As they got closer, they saw restraints at his hands and feet.

"Why did they put him in restraints?" asked McKenna.

Therese didn't answer that directly. "Clint," she said. "Do you think you can help him?

Clint walked to the bedside and noticed that, despite the man's white hair, his skin was not wrinkled as a man in his 80's or so would be. He might have been in his early thirties. "Who is he?" he asked.

"Steve Blair," said Therese. "My dad hired him as captain of his yacht. The South African Coast Guard found it floating derelict off the Cape of Good Hope. Something terrified the other crew members so that they're struggling to talk about what happened. My father seems okay, but he's being very strange. He doesn't seem to be affected at all, except he can't tell us what happened."

Clint took the hand of the man lying on the bed.

CHAPTER NINE

Clint found himself on the bridge of a yacht, a motor launch, struggling in high waves. The vessel was trying to round The Cape of Good Hope, despite the dark, the difficult currents, and the huge swells.

Clint understood that he was seeing what the captain of the yacht was seeing and that he'd just had an humiliating encounter with the owner of the vessel, whose name was McNulty.

"Sir," said one of the crewmen, approaching. "Barometer's continuing to drop. We're not too far from the Cape Town harbor. Shouldn't we head there? This is a screamer," he concluded.

Steve shrugged. "Mr. McNulty says go on through," he said. "It's his ship."

"Sir?" said another crewman. "There's a small boat off the port side. Looks like one man in it…"

Clint drew back into his own mind. What happened with that small boat terrified the man in the bed. Now Clint went back into the other man's mind. "Steve?" he called.

No answer. "Steve!"

No answer. "Steve, come back," said Clint. "You're hiding. I know it's terrifying. I think I can help."

At last. "Who are you?" asked a small, frightened voice, like that of a little boy.

"I'm Dr. Clint Byrne," said Clint. "I'm a close friend of the McNulty family."

"How can you be talking to me?" asked the voice.

"I'm using a rare gift called the Cymreig," said Clint. "I'm a descendant of the Irish Faeraes."

"Fairy?"

"That's what they're called in mythology, yes," said Clint. "But I assure you I'm real."

Clouds of white whispered around Clint Byrne. He wasn't afraid. He had dealt with this before, though never had he gone so far into another man's soul.

"What do you want?" asked the voice.

"I want you to come back," said Clint. "You're in a hospital. You're safe. We can help you face what's terrified you into this retreat."

"You cannot do this," said Steve, as if he couldn't believe it.

"Yes, I think I can," said Clint. "And you have to trust me. My wife and I are both trained psychologists. Besides that, your muscles have begun to atrophy. If you don't begin to reverse things you won't be able to turn it around. I'm afraid you'll die weak and helpless. Come on. I won't hurt you."

Silence for several heartbeats. "You don't know what I saw," said the voice of Steve Blair's soul.

"Whatever you saw," said Clint, "I can help you face it. Come on."

He held out his hand. A few moments later someone took hold and Clint backed away, emerging from the mind of the other person—

Then he stood next to the bed, his wife embracing him.

"Clint," she whispered. "Are you all right?"

"Yes," said Clint. "How's Steve?"

The man on the bed began to stir. He opened his eyes and they fell on Therese McNulty. "Miss McNulty," Steve began. "I—"

"It's okay, Steve," said Therese. "You're safe." She took his hand and held it between hers.

"Are you Clint?" asked Steve, looking at Clint and then at his wife. Clint nodded. "Did you say you are a doctor?"

"We both are," said Clint, "though not medical doctors. My wife and I both have our doctorates."

"In Psychology?" said Steve.

"Yes," said McKenna. "How do you feel?"

A moment or two passed as Steve evaluated his body. "I'm okay," he said. "Where's the crew?"

"On the *Arcturus*," said Therese. "Everyone's okay. My father's here and he seems a little strange."

Steve nodded. "How long have I been here?" he asked.

"Five days," said Therese. "Do you remember what happened on *Arcturus*?

Steve thought. "Some of it," he said. "Something strange happened, but I don't remember much of it."

"I think you're blocking something," said Clint.

"You may be right," said Steve. "When I start to go down a certain path, I get terrified and have to stop."

Therese said, "It must have been terrible." She looked at Clint and McKenna. "I can tell you Steve's no coward."

Clint nodded. "I could sense that."

"We could try hypnotism," said McKenna. "But I don't think I want to go there right now."

"Can I get up?" asked Steve.

"We'll ask the doctors," Therese said. "I think you ought to rest for a while before we get at that, though."

"I can't take any more dreaming," said Steve.

McKenna looked at Clint. He blinked and gave a little shrug. "I do know something scared him in the midst of a storm on the Cape, but I couldn't get at it."

"Steve?" said Therese. "Can you tell us what terrified you?"

Tears started in the man's eyes. "I want to, Miss McNulty," he said. "I just can't go there right now."

At that moment a doctor came in and started in surprise to see Steve awake. "Excellent," he said. "I feared the coma would last for some time." He turned to the people standing next to the bed. "Will you give me the room?" he said. "I really need to examine Captain Blair."

"Steve, we'll come back in a little while," said Therese. "I want to take Clint to see my father."

The doctor turned to Clint. "Are you a Physician, sir?" he asked.

"I am a doctor," said Clint, "though not in medicine. I have a Ph. D. in clinical psychology."

The doctor nodded. "Please excuse me for a few moments."

"One thing," said Therese. "Could you give him an anesthetic that would allow him to sleep without dreaming?"

"Yes," said the doctor. "I will prescribe one."

Therese leaned over the bed and hugged Steve Blair. The hug lingered and McKenna shot a glance at her husband. Both of them raised their eyebrows.

"We'll see you in a little while," said Therese. "Try to get some sleep, will you?"

Steve Blair smiled at her and reached up a hand. Therese took it and held it for a brief moment to her face.

Therese smiled and waved at Steve as they left the room. "Er," said McKenna. "Did something just happen between you and Steve?"

"Well, let's say that I would have been devastated if he'd died there," said Therese, smiling. "I've had a crush on him for a few years, but I always figured nothing would come of it." She led them into a room and found Mac McNulty staring out the window.

"Dad?" said Therese. The man turned.

In all her life, McKenna Byrne had never seen such an evil countenance. The eyes bored into her, as if searching for her soul, with the perfect intent of destroying it. The eyes might have been blue, but they seemed like blade steel as they roved over the group.

McNulty spoke. "What do you want?" he hissed.

"Dad, it's me," said Therese. "It's Therese. These are my friends. You've met McKenna, my college roommate, you remember. She's married to this man, Clint Byrne."

The man gave a snort and turned back to the window. "What is this place?" he asked.

"It's called a hospital," Therese nodded. "A house for healing."

"Where?" asked the man.

"Cape Town," said Therese. The man didn't reply. "The Republic of South Africa? The Cape of Good Hope?" The man showed not a glimmer of recognition.

"Something's wrong here," said Clint in an aside to his wife. She nodded.

"Can you check it out?" McKenna whispered.

"I'm not sure I want to," he admitted. "But I'll try." He walked to the window. He stretched out his hand. The man hesitated, but then gave him his hand.

Chapter Ten

Clint slid through the man's eyes into his mind. "Who are you?" he asked.

The man hesitated, as if searching through his soul. "McNulty," said the man after a pause. "How are you talking to me?"

"I'm using an old Irish mind trick called The Cymreig," said Clint.

"Well, get out of my mind," snarled the other. "You have no right—"

"I'm not really speaking to Mac McNulty, am I," said Clint.

"What do you mean?"

"I mean, your body, your voice, your mannerisms appear to be those of McNulty," returned Clint. "But in the deepest part of you, whatever makes Mac McNulty a distinct and separate individual is not you."

"That's absurd," said the man.

"Really," said Clint. He walked deeper into the man's mind—

And fell into a nightmare.

CHAPTER ELEVEN

The ship heeled and bucked as forty to fifty foot swells over took it and crashed into it. The captain bellowed orders and the sailors did their best, but the ship floundered in clear distress. "Captain," said Clint, though that was not his name here. "Let's make for the coast. We may yet survive."

"No," shouted the Captain. "We'll round the Horn in a few hours. Full sail!" he shrieked.

A gigantic swell washed over the ship. One man screamed in terror as the wind and sea tore his grip on a rope away and he washed into the sea.

"Never mind!" shouted the Captain. "We'll make it!"

The captain leaped for the rigging and nimble as he was, ascended to the top of the main mast. Clint heard what sounded like terrible blasphemies and curses hurled at heaven over the scream of the hurricane force winds—and then everything changed.

Clint backed out of the man's mind.

"My God," he said and the term was a prayer. "All those men—"

"What happened, Clint?" asked McKenna.

He turned to Therese. "Therese," he mumbled. "Maybe you should sit down."

CHAPTER TWELVE

cKenna, Therese and Clint walked out of the hospital room. They found a lounge not far down the hall. "What is it, Clint?" asked Therese.

He took a deep breath. "Therese," he said. "Look, this is going to sound crazy."

"What?" said Therese, as she gave McKenna a nervous glance.

"Whatever it is that makes Mac McNulty an individual is gone from this person," said Clint. "Somehow, someone stole his soul and replaced it in his body."

Therese stared, her expression blank and dumbfounded. "What?" she managed.

"I warned you that this would sound crazy," said Clint. "But I'm completely serious. This man looks just like your father, but he's a seaman from a ship called *Der Fleigende Hollander*. He's taken your father's soul and replaced it with his."

"What does the ship's name mean?" asked McKenna.

"When you translate from the Dutch," said Clint. "I'm pretty sure that it means *The Flying Dutchman*."

For several seconds the two young women stared at Clint, their faces blank with inability to respond. "The—" stammered Therese.

"You heard me right," said Clint. "*The Flying Dutchman*. A

myth, a story, a legend, right. But I know that whatever makes your father a distinct and separate individual from everyone else on earth has either vanished or been buried away so deep as to be inaccessible."

The three stood in silence for a few moments. McKenna put her arm around her friend.

"Can this be possible?" asked Therese.

"I don't know how he did it," said Clint. "All I know is that somehow your father is not living inside his body. I don't know if your father is alive or dead, either."

"What do we do?" asked Therese. "Can the process be reversed?"

"I haven't a clue," said Clint. "I've never seen anything like this. I think that he swapped souls with your dad. I mean, he put his soul inside your dad and your dad now lives inside him."

"Something like demonic possession?" asked McKenna.

Clint frowned. "No, not quite," he said. "This person—I mean, the man who came aboard--is evil, beyond a doubt. To take someone else's soul is evil. I have the feeling that this person selected your father because he sensed something is wrong with your father and that he's going to die soon."

Again a silence. "Therese?" said McKenna. "Is your dad sick?"

Therese hesitated. "It's possible," she admitted. "He's been seeing a lot of doctors back home. Whenever I asked him what's wrong, he's vague. I tried to contact his family doctor, but he wouldn't talk to me. Something about confidentiality."

McKenna nodded. "Yes, that could be a problem in the U.S."

"Could you ask this man?" asked Therese.

"Let's try," agreed Clint.

They walked back into the room and saw the man standing across the room, staring out the window. He turned and his expression again reflected fury. "What do you want?"

"I know," said Clint.

Silence descended on the room for several seconds. At last, the man snarled, "What do you think you know?"

"I know that you aren't McNulty," said Clint. "I know that you're someone else."

"That's ridiculous," said the man.

"No, it isn't," said Clint, keeping his voice under control. "I don't know how you did it, but somehow, his soul – I mean, whatever it is that makes Mac McNulty a distinct individual from everyone else -- is not in his body. You are someone else, someone who has been lost for years – no, centuries -- and who has survived under a curse, unable to die or even to become ill."

Silence. "You have access to all his memories," said Clint. "For example you know how to speak English, all about his businesses, his family and many other things. But you can't hide your soul."

"What else?" sneered the man.

"Why did you do it?" asked Therese.

"This inquisition is absurd," said the man. "Get out or I'll have you thrown out."

"Where is Mac McClelland?" persisted Clint.

The man snorted. He crossed to the bed and pushed the button to summon the nurse. "We're not going," said Therese. "Not until we get some answers."

A nurse appeared at the door. "May I help you?"

The man gave an imperious wave. "These people are

annoying me," he said. "Throw them out."

Clint turned to the nurse, who started to speak, but then stopped when she looked into his eyes. A moment later she spoke. "Please, sir," she said. "These people mean you no harm. Relax and let them talk to you." She turned and left the room.

"The Cymreig?" smiled McKenna. Clint nodded.

"What did you do?" asked the man.

"Never mind," said Clint. "Now answer the question or I'll take it from you."

The man's bravado began to crumple. He tried to bluster, but Clint brushed it aside. At last the man surrendered. "My name is Oosterhuis," he said.

"Ah," said Therese. "It's true."

"Why did you take this man's soul?" asked Clint.

"Because he's going to die," said Oosterhuis.

"He's going to die?" cried Therese. "How would you know that?"

"I don't know how I know it," said Oosterhuis. "But I do know it, and I can tell you that this person understands that his body is going to die, and it won't be pleasant."

"Do you mean that you've offered to suffer in his place?" said McKenna.

"That's right," Oosterhuis nodded. "That's the offer I made."

"What does he get in return?" asked Clint. "He's agreed to take your place on *The Dutchman,* but what could persuade anyone to make such a deal?"

"He doesn't die," shrugged Oosterhuis.

"Ever?" said Therese when she was able to speak. Oosterhuis nodded. "You mean he can never die?" she stammered, confused and unable to comprehend.

"That's right," nodded Oosterhuis. "The ship and all its crew are doomed to sail the Cape until Judgment Day."

"But what kind of a life is that?" cried McKenna. "Why would anyone agree to that?"

"I am not such a person," said Oosterhuis. "I became on that ship through no decision on my part. No choice was offered me in the matter. But on occasion someone makes a deal with one of us, as I did with your father. I took over his being and all of his substance."

"But you know nothing about the business, nothing about how his life works—"

"That's true," shrugged Oosterhuis. "But irrelevant. I simply retire, take as much money as I need, and live out this body's life. Which won't be long," he added.

"Don't you have any fear of God?" asked McKenna. Oosterhuis shrugged. "Will He forgive this theft?" McKenna demanded.

"You don't understand, even now," said the sailor. "I gave McNulty eternal life. He won't die. He'll live on the ship forever."

"Is it as wonderful as it sounds?" said McKenna sarcastically.

"For someone as afraid of death as he is, yes," said Oosterhuis.

Therese made a little choking sound, and then left the room with a suddenness that surprised her friends. The exit made Oosterhuis chuckle.

Clint looked hard at Oosterhuis. "Are you in a great deal of pain?"

"Why do you ask?" snarled Oosterhuis. "I am in control."

"Yes," said Clint. "But not for long. The cancer you have will be desperately painful."

Now the brash coarseness of the man's expression softened for a second and Clint saw the wince. He crossed to the bedside table and picked up a small plastic bottle.

"Have you taken any of these?" he asked Oosterhuis.

"No," returned the sailor. "What do you mean?"

Clint poured a glass of water and shook one of the tablets out of them. He directed Oosterhuis in how to swallow it.

"Look," he said. "You know how to use the buzzer. Do you know how to summon the nurse?"

Oosterhuis nodded. He gave evidence of extreme emotion and some fear. Clint put a hand on his shoulder and a gentle squeeze.

Chapter Thirteen

few moments later McKenna and Clint found their friend Therese in the hallway.

"Clint," she said. "Is this true? Can it really be possible?"

"It seems like it's true," he said. "This person, despite what he looks like, is certainly not Mac McNulty. How they accomplished this is beyond me, however."

"Me too," said Therese. "Besides the way he looks, I see nothing whatever of my father. And I don't think I have a way in the world of stopping him from taking Dad's money, his property, anything."

Clint shrugged. "We could try to negotiate something--"

"Like what?" said Therese.

"I don't know, maybe give him an allowance—"

"But the businesses—" said Therese.

"Well, could you take over?" asked McKenna.

"I don't have his experience, his skills, his knowledge," sighed Therese.

Clint looked up. "I think we need to go and get your father," he said. "We need to rescue him from this hell on earth."

"You mean we have to go and find a ghost ship?" said McKenna.

"Well," said Clint, "I don't think this man is going to survive very long. He's going to die, soon and hard. If we don't find your father, he'll be lost on a death ship forever."

Therese looked at him. "I don't know if I have the courage to go on an expedition like that," she said.

"None of us has that kind of courage," said McKenna. "No one can look into the face of supernatural evil alone."

"What do we do, then?" asked her friend.

"We face it together," said McKenna. "We'll stand right with you." She took Clint's hand and embraced Therese's shoulders.

They walked down the hall to Steve Blair's room. They found him sitting on the edge of the bed, dressed, showered and shaved. He looked alive again.

"Steve," smiled Therese. "You look much better."

"Yeah, I feel fine," he said. "Look, I want to apologize for…"

"You have nothing to apologize for," asserted Therese.

Steve started to speak, but stopped. "Well, thanks," he said. "But I should have done a better job of protecting your father. He trusted me to get the ship through and I didn't."

"He didn't know the risk?" asked Clint.

Steve hesitated. "Miss McNulty, please forgive me for saying this," he said. "He gave me the impression that he felt he couldn't be hurt."

"But he's dying," said McKenna.

"The cancer," nodded Steve. "Well, yes, but I think he felt that he'd overcome that in the end. He'd never faced a situation he couldn't fix by himself, I guess, and…"

An uncomfortable silence settled in. "I think I understand," said Clint.

"What do you mean?" asked Therese.

McKenna nodded in agreement with her husband. "You see

it with people who have a lot of success, or adulation heaped on them," she said. "Consider, say, the American movie stars of the thirties."

"Or sports stars, or the very wealthy," nodded Clint.

McKenna agreed. "Many of them made so much money, so fast, and had so much adoration and attention from fans that they began to think that they were something more than just human."

Therese stood, considering for a few moments. "I can see that," said Therese. "Many times I felt I didn't even know my father. He'd be there in body, but not present otherwise. He didn't think he had to obey any laws."

McKenna gave a little nod. "When I was teaching, my high school had a school cop, a liaison to the Village police force, named Tad Jamieson. I was eating lunch with him one day when he told me that he'd made a traffic stop over the weekend on a fabulous sports car, a Ferrari, red of course. The owner got out."

"Oh brother," said Steve. "I can see this coming."

"Right," said McKenna. "Tad didn't identify him to me by name, but he said the driver owned a famous restaurant in the town. When Tad asked for his license, the driver got arrogant and very superior. The driver asked Todd, 'Do you know who I am?'"

"Uh, oh," said Therese.

"Yeah, you never want to say that to a cop," smiled McKenna. "The next thing this guy knows, he's at the police station, cuffed, booked and fingerprinted. Someone had to come and bail him out. Of course, that meant court, a stiff fine, his car towed and impounded, and he had to face some pretty serious and very public humiliation. A terrific hassle, to say the least."

"On the other hand, sometimes people get away with such arrogance their whole life," said Steve.

"And that's what happened with my father?" asked Therese.

"Well, I wouldn't say your father got away with it," said Steve. "But yes, he'd come to the point that not even the forces of nature alarmed him. He thought he couldn't be touched by the weather of the cape."

"Victor Fleming, the director of *The Wizard of Oz*, said something at the close of production of the movie," smiled Clint. "He's supposed to have said, 'I'd like to thank all the little people.'"

"Did he mean the Munchkins?" said McKenna.

"Well, maybe," Clint chuckled. "Anyhow, sometimes it happens. People with too much money, too much adulation, too much material stuff, can sometimes come to believe that they're something more than merely human."

"But Dad knew he was going to die—" began Therese, but then stopped.

"Therese?" said McKenna when her friend didn't go on.

"I think I get it," said Therese. "He thought that he could outsmart death. If he joined *The Flying Dutchman* crew, he could go on forever. Never die."

"On a ghost ship?" cried McKenna. "Never touching land, never accomplishing anything, replaying the same events over and over--"

"Sounds like a vision of Hell to me," said Clint.

"No," said Therese, shaking her head. "You don't understand how Dad thinks. He'd beyond question figure that he'd go aboard the ship, displace the captain, rule the roost as he did everywhere he went in life, and—well, he'd get used to it.

"Isn't there a legend about the gold of the *Dutchman*?" asked Steve.

"As I recall, the *Dutchman* set out loaded down with gold," nodded Clint. "Also spices and silks from the Far East, India and perhaps China as well."

"Surely it must have sunk long since," said Therese.

"That would be logical, I agree," said Steve, and Clint nodded.

"Maybe so," said McKenna. "But I recall that it's been sighted dozens of times since the middle of the sixteenth century."

"A ghost ship, then," said Therese.

"Well, yes," said McKenna. "But that can't possibly be true…" now she paused.

"Well, you've dealt with the supernatural before," smiled Clint.

"Yes," she said. "But a whole ship of ghosts? That seems ridiculous. I think."

Chapter Fourteen

After a bit more conversation, McKenna and Clint left Therese and had a cab take them to the Red Carnation hotel. They found their room, a beautiful suite overlooking the ocean, and decided a nap would not come by any means amiss.

After a two hour nap, the jet lag eased and they relaxed in the room for some time, talking over their experiences in the trip. Then, they showered and cleaned up for the evening.

Therese and Steve joined them for dinner in the hotel at a stunning restaurant called Azure. Though expensive, the dinner remained consistent with the fine cuisine McKenna had enjoyed in the country so far.

"What do we do now?" asked McKenna, as they lingered over a glass of the fine South African wine the sommelier had recommended. It had a remarkable texture, and McKenna said that it was like drinking a fine velvet.

Therese turned to Steve. "Do you think you'll be able to help us?" she asked.

"Maybe so, yes," he said. "I'll do what I can. If we can get *Arcturus* ready, we can take it."

Therese shrugged her shoulders. "From what the harbor police told me, it didn't sustain any damage," she said. "We'll need to stock it up, of course."

"How long?" asked McKenna.

"I'd say less than a week, wouldn't you, Steve?" she asked.

He nodded, but looked rather pale. "I don't know what we can do," he said. "But I guess we can try. A couple of days, I should think."

"Why don't you two do some sight-seeing for a few days?" Therese told McKenna and Clint, as she grabbed the check. "I can take care of stuff here. I also need to get some time off from work."

"Is that a problem?" asked Clint.

"No," she said. "I haven't taken a vacation since I've been with the company. I think I could use one now."

"Agreed," said McKenna.

CHAPTER FIFTEEN

Clint and McKenna slept well in their room at the Red Carnation that night and in the morning did some sight-seeing in Cape Town. They rented a car and took another tour of the city and went into the nearby countryside. They took a cable car to the top of Table Mountain and sat on the edge of the cliff on a beautiful day. The majestic view of the Cape of Good Hope stunned them.

McKenna linked her arm through her husband's arm and leaned her head against his shoulder. He turned to her and kissed the top of her head. "Well, what have we gotten ourselves into this time?" asked Clint.

"I know, I know," said McKenna. "But Therese really loves her father. I can identify."

"I've never met him," said Clint.

"I have," McKenna nodded. "He's a guy whose parents didn't have much use for him. I think all the money has evolved into his way of keeping score."

"Keeping score?" smiled Clint.

"I mean he's trying to show everyone how great he is," said McKenna. "He wants to be remembered as a vastly wealthy man, someone who could order others around, hire and fire—the ultimate in power grabs."

"And he figures he's even cheated death," murmured Clint.

"He thinks."

"Well, you've read all the sea stories I have," shrugged McKenna. "*Mutiny on the Bounty*, the Hornblower stories, the Patrick O'Brian yarns, and so on."

"Sure," he said. "Some of my favorite stories."

"But these ships were scarcely paradises," McKenna said. "Hollywood tried to show what the life was like in some cases, but couldn't make them as awful as they really were."

"Authors and filmmakers can't even come close," he said. "The lives those mariners led must have been awful. Dangerous, hard labor; away from home for months; brutal discipline—on and on."

"Yes, and life at sea can be tough even today," his wife nodded.

"This whole thing transcends the natural order," said Clint. "But then, so does the Cymreig, I guess. Maybe I can help. I know I have to try."

"Dr. Byrne?" said a voice behind them.

Both husband and wife turned and saw a man in jeans, a hooded sweatshirt and jogging shoes standing behind them. "We're both named Dr. Byrne," said McKenna, smiling and extending her hand. She introduced herself to the man.

The man nodded and shook their hands. "My name is Clovis," he said. "May I please have a word with you?"

"Of course," said Clint. Some minutes later, Clint and McKenna ordered a couple of glasses of wine at a small table at an outdoor café. The man named Clovis joined them and ordered a small tomato juice. "Please," he said. "My English would not, on my best days, be considered without flaw. I speak Afrikaans almost exclusively. Do not hesitate to ask me to explain something I've said."

Clint and McKenna were amused at his self-deprecation and assured him that his communication didn't bother them at all.

"How can we help you?" asked McKenna when they had sipped at their drinks.

The man held up a finger and glanced around the outdoor café. "I have been sent to warn you."

Husband and wife exchanged glances. "Warn us about what?" asked Clint.

"You intend to go after Mr. McNulty," he said, and it was a statement.

Clint and McKenna exchanged glances. They'd thought they were being somewhat confidential. "How did you know that?" asked McKenna.

"I didn't," said the man. "My father told me."

Again the husband and wife exchanged glances. "How did your father know?" asked Clint.

"As you Americans like to say, 'it's complicated,' smiled the man. "But my father knows this sort of thing."

"What sort of thing?" asked McKenna, bewildered. "I'm sorry, Sir, but I'm really quite confused. How do you know us? What do you want?"

The man drew a deep breath. "My family have always been fishermen," he said. "Some time ago, my father, my uncle and my father's best friend, named Vincent, went out to fish in the early morning." He gestured in the general direction of the harbor.

"They wanted to fish off the Cape of Good Hope?" said Clint, a wry expression on his face.

"Yes," said Clovis. "Many people do, of course. They had a

stout craft, owned by my father's best friend and they had done it many times."

"Go on," said McKenna.

"They had some success through the morning," said Clovis. "And the day remained beautiful. But then a cloud engulfed them, appearing as suddenly as if someone had thrown a switch. The wind increased and it grew dark, well before the sun would have gone down. These were experienced sailors, of course, and they had dealt with rough weather many times. As a result they were not particularly frightened. However, as they turned to make for home, a ship appeared between them and the harbor."

"A ship?" said Clint.

"Yes," said Clovis. "And not just any ship. This ship seemed to be bathed in a golden light. It moved, it seemed, at its own will, irrespective of the wind and the current. As the ship pulled alongside, they made out the name on the prow. Perhaps you can guess?"

"*Der Fleigende Hollander*," nodded Clint.

"Exactly," nodded Clovis.

"And what happened?" Clint asked.

"They don't know, or, perhaps to be a bit more accurate, none of them could remember," Clovis said and sipped at his tea.

A silence settled over the group. McKenna spoke up at last. "But your father survived?"

"Yes, and so did my grandfather," said Clovis. "And so, they thought, did their friend, whose name was Klein. My father and grandfather have no memory of the next two hours, and Klein said he didn't, either. Let me assure you, these are good, honest men."

"So they don't have any idea what happened during those two hours?" asked Clint.

"That's it precisely," said Clovis. "They woke up—if that's the right word—as they were about to enter to Cape Town harbor. They have no memory of what happened from the moment they saw the rope ladder lowered until they were nearly docked. Their fish were still in the kreels, their poles were baited, the sun had come back out and a gentle wind propelled the craft."

"Good grief," said McKenna. "What happened after they got back?"

"Well, Dad and Grandpa were okay, but their friend became strange from the time they met the Ship on," said Clovis. "He would start to cry tears that my Dad has always said were tears of fear, if not terror. His appetite declined, he lost a great deal of weight and in general seemed to waste away."

"Hm," said McKenna. "How long did this go on?"

"From what my father said, two or two and one-half years," said Clovis. "Yes, they went fishing almost every day as usual. Then, one morning Mr. Klein…er…vanished. Flick. Like that," he said, snapping his fingers. "No one saw him leave, he told no one where he was going, but one morning, he just disappeared. No one has ever seen him again."

"Could he have gone inland?" asked McKenna.

Clovis shook his head. "It has been on the disappearance and legend story boards at the wharf since he disappeared," he said. "I need to tell you that a small boat vanished that day also."

"Yes?" said Steve.

"Yes," said Clovis. "The owner reported it to the Coast

Guard, but the boat was small, inconsequential except of course to its owner, and the community presumed it lost at sea. Fishing boats went out, as did the Coast Guard, and Air Rescue. The boat had vanished also, presumed lost at sea.

"I hear a 'but' coming," said McKenna.

Clovis nodded. "Yesterday I saw the boat for the first time in years," he said. "Since Mr. Klein vanished."

McKenna and Clint stared at Clovis for a few seconds. Clint recovered to ask, "May I guess?"

Clovis nodded. "Did you see it lashed to *Arcturus*?" asked McKenna.

"Yes," said Clovis. "I did."

"So it sounds like your friend went aboard the *Dutchman*, doesn't it," nodded Clint.

"Yes, well, it's possible," shrugged Clovis. "I don't know if he's a prisoner, or even if he's alive, or what may have happened. For that matter I don't know how you got the boat."

Clint and McKenna didn't know how to respond. At last Clint managed, "The boat drifted alongside *Arcturus*, our yacht." Clovis nodded. "So—ah—what should we do?" Asked Clint.

Clovis shrugged. "I believe we can find a way to end the curse of *Der Fleigende Hollander*," he said. "Yes, it is a curse. But I think we might be able to find someone who is part of the crew, someone who may know about the curse, and who will see a path to end the curse."

"In other words, I couldn't board the ship," said Clint.

Clovis shook his head. "I think that yes, you might be able to get aboard," said Clovis. "I have nothing to go on except legends and what my grandpa and my dad used to tell me. But you mustn't go aboard. They will take your soul."

"What do you mean?" asked McKenna.

"If you should find the ship, you will find yourselves in appalling danger," said Clovis. "Keep yourselves in prayer, please. The only way to escape the ship, it seems, is to find someone who will trade lives with you. If you don't do it of your own free will, they will steal it, that is, take it by force."

They promised and took Clovis' personal business card, and agreed to let him know what had happened with the expedition.

As the man turned to go, McKenna felt a strong leading to speak up. "Mr. Clovis," said McKenna. Clovis turned beck. "Sir, would you like to come with us?"

Clovis hesitated. "Thank you," he said. "It is gracious of you. But I'm. . ." he paused.

"Afraid?" guessed Clint.

"Yes," admitted Clovis. "There are few incidents recorded in history where eternity and real life intersect. Once in a while it occurs, however."

"Like when an angel appears?" smiled Clint.

"Yes, that's it exactly," agreed Clovis. "In those moments, people find themselves in the intersection between this world and the immortal. That truly frightens most of the people to whom it happens."

"Right," said Clint. "Angels always begin their visits by saying, 'Don't be afraid.'"

"That's right," agreed Clovis.

Clint and McKenna made arrangements to meet Clovis near the ship in the morning. He left, promising to pack for cold weather as well.

Clint and McKenna walked around in downtown Cape Town for a while, purchasing presents to send home to relatives and friends. They talked about what they were discovering.

"Do you think someone wants us to find *The Dutchman*?" mused McKenna.

"That's pretty enigmatic," said her husband with a smile.

"I know," she said. "But don't you think some pretty strange things have happened?"

"We have had quite a few coincidences, I agree. How did Clovis know what we were doing?"

McKenna thought. "Well, he did say his father told him," she said.

Clint shrugged. "Of course, that begs the question, how did *he* know?"

McKenna bit her lip and gave her head a little shake.

Chapter Sixteen

That night, McKenna and Clint met their friends for dinner at a restaurant near the Cape Town port. They sat outside with a view of the harbor and watched massive cranes loading freight boxes onto ships. "The dock works around the clock, lights and all," said Clint. Steve nodded as they watched.

"What did you learn about the *Arcturus*?" asked McKenna.

"I think we're ready," said Steve.

"The weather is going to be as good as it gets for the next week, Mickey," said her friend Therese. "Steve would like to sail tomorrow, in fact."

"So you got the ship provisioned and so on?" asked Clint.

"Yeah," said Steve. "But to describe what we have as a skeleton crew would be a crime against truth in advertising." They all looked at Steve and listened to his explanation.

"These guys are experienced sailors," said Steve. "But what we saw scared them to distraction, also. I don't think they want to face what we saw again. We paid them off and sent them home."

"Then why does Clovis want to come?" asked McKenna.

"I can't imagine," said Steve. The waitress appeared and they ordered dinner.

* * * * *

Steve and Therese prepared the ship to sail the next morning. When Clovis arrived, Clint and McKenna introduced him to Therese and Steve who made him welcome. They gave him a bunk in the crew quarters.

"Do you have a cook on board?" Clovis asked.

"No," Steve said. "We thought we'd take turns, though."

"I used to work in a restaurant as a cook," Clovis grinned. "If I can help, why…"

"That would be great," exclaimed Therese and McKenna in unison. Clint and Steve chuckled with Clovis at their enthusiasm.

"Okay," he said. "I'd better get to work on serving out lunch."

In mid-morning, Steve and Clint cast off and the ship began making her way out of the harbor with deliberate speed. "Where do we go?" asked McKenna.

Steve pointed to a map. "Here," he said. "From here, we'll make something of a spiral search grid."

"How far is it to Antarctica?"

"Several hundred miles," said Steve. "I hope we don't have to go there, that's for sure."

"Did you stay close to the shoreline?" asked Clint. "When you left Durban, I mean?"

"As much as possible," he agreed. "In fact, we weren't far from Cape Town when…it…whatever it was happened. Why?"

"Just a thought," said Clint. "When a ship from that era rounded the Cape, would she also stay as close to the shore as possible?"

"I would assume so," nodded Steve. "Those would be the

current shipping lanes, also. I can't think of a reason to go to Antarctica unless you were on a scientific expedition of some sort. No one lives there except penguins, you have to deal with the hideous weather, of course, and it's pretty forbidding."

"If a ship from that era got lost," asked McKenna, "could it make its way down there?"

"I suppose it's possible," said Steve. "Are you saying we should look for the *Dutchman* near Antarctica?"

"Okay, say it is a ghost ship, like the legends say," said McKenna. "Most people feel that ghosts are the last manifestation of humans trapped in a warp of doing something over and over again, ensnared in an endless loop of utter futility, unable to achieve a goal, but determined to do so."

Steve thought. "But Oosterhuis, the crewman who came from the *Dutchman* knew the ship was dead, somehow," he said. "I wonder if they've figured out what is going on after all these years."

"Is it possible they've always known it?" asked Theresa.

"What do you mean?" asked Steve.

Theresa shrugged. "One definition of insanity says that it consists in doing the same thing the same way over and over, hoping that you'll achieve a different result."

"Yes," said McKenna. "I've heard that too."

"Yeah," said Clint. "Sort of reminds you of Chicago baseball fans."

"Come on," said McKenna. "The White Sox won the World Series in 2005."

"Yeah," said Clint. "And the Cubs won a World Series in what, 1908? I think it's been over a hundred years for sure." He gave a wink to the others. "Not *quite* as long as the *Dutchman*'s been missing."

"Well, yeah, they won it all at the start of the twentieth century," said McKenna. "But lay off, will you? Any team can have a bad century."

That night, after Clovis served them a fine dinner, Steve left the table and returned in a few moments. He sat with the group, which included Clovis, in the ship's dining room, spread a nautical map on the table and pointed.

"Look," he said. "I did a search over the last few days. I tried to establish a grid showing where sightings of the *Dutchman* have taken place here in these waters. It's sort of interesting."

The group peered over his shoulder. The sightings made something of a pattern, all of it leading down toward Antarctica. "Here," said Steve. "Let's disregard the legends of sightings in Australia, or in England, or like that. People describe *The Dutchman* as a spectre in these appearances, from all I can tell. In the sightings near the Cape, the ship seems to be a lot more clearly defined."

"I don't follow this," said McKenna.

"Look," said Steve. "Something happened on that ship. Legend says that the Captain cursed God. Okay. His soul may be damned—we have no way of telling—but cursing God isn't fatal, as far as I know. You don't die when you curse God, do you?"

McKenna thought through the Bible. "People who die usually are doing blasphemous things, like Ananias and Sapphira in the books of Acts. They withheld money and lied about it, and then they dropped dead. I don't know—"

"I take Steve's point," said Clint. "According to legend, the ship was *in extremis*, right? The Captain went up into the crosstrees in a wild storm. He could have been killed by falling, by lightning, washed over the side—"

"Something's wrong here," said McKenna. "If everyone died in that storm, how do we know that story?"

"That's the precise point," said Steve. "I think some, at least one, of the sailors escaped the ship before it foundered."

"And that sailor or whatever number of shipmates made it back to the coast, found a way to get to another port, and told the story of the *Dutchman* to receptive ears—"

"Receptive and, it seems pretty likely, a bit skeptical and even superstitious, right?" said Therese.

Steve nodded. "I'm guessing that the sailors made up a fine story about a shipwreck, a vast untold horde of treasure lost forever, and a ghost ship."

"So they wouldn't be hanged for desertion?" asked Clint.

"Yeah, maybe," agreed Steve. "But that would also give them a reason for salvage as well."

McKenna thought for a while. "Oh," she said. "The gold."

"Right," said Steve.

"But no one has ever tried to salvage the *Dutchman*, right?" asked McKenna.

"Not that I can find," said Steve. "I imagine that it's at the bottom of the ocean. Salvage would be pretty tough, if not downright impossible. The seas and the weather would be prohibitive."

"We're overlooking something," said Clint. "Oosterhuis." The others were silent, pondering his words.

"I'm not forgetting him," said Steve. "Somehow he made his way to our boat and hijacked your dad, Therese."

"Oosterhuis?" said Clovis, speaking up for the first time.

Clint explained about the seaman who had taken over Mac's body.

"That's the story we heard from Oosterhuis, anyhow," said Therese. "But it sounds like Dad was willing to be hijacked. It seems pretty strange that such a thing can be accomplished even in the spirit world."

"Now I'm starting to get scared," said McKenna. "Are we talking demonic forces?"

"Have you ever heard of God allowing a spirit to occupy another person?" asked Therese.

"You mean, like in *The Exorcist or Rosemary's Baby?*" asked Clint.

"Well, C. S. Lewis wrote *The Screwtape Letters*, as you know," said McKenna. "The book purports to be a series of letters from a senior devil to a junior apprentice demon. I recall reading that when he finished the book, Lewis went into a retreat for many months, trying to stop thinking as a demon would think."

"I also heard that the actors who play Screwtape in the stage plays do the same thing after they finish the run of the show," said Clint. "But do you know of God allowing possession?" he asked his wife.

"Well, no," said McKenna. "There's a story in Acts about Paul driving out a demon from a woman named Tabitha. But the demon hadn't stolen her soul or replaced it with something else, just crippled her ability to function."

"Yeah, and Jesus drove out the demons who called themselves 'Legion'," Clint nodded. "But again, the man was still in there, just submerged by the multiplicity of demons."

"Are we saying that this man Oosterhuis is a demon?" asked Therese.

"No, I don't think so," said McKenna. "But he's been kept alive—such as he is—for this very thing, I think."

Steve mused about this. "Yeah, there's some reason," he said. "But can Mac McNulty be any worse than a demon?"

"What do you mean?" asked Therese. "Remember, you're talking about my father. He may have been power hungry with so much to prove, but a demon? I don't think so."

"I don't mean to offend you," said Steve. "But in all my work experience I've never met someone as arrogant, demanding and demeaning as your father. If a demon can be worse than him to work for, I don't know how."

"Are you saying people won't know the difference?" asked Clint.

"Oosterhuis plans to die in peace," said McKenna.

"The key word, though, is 'plans'," said Clint. "Who's to say he's going to go gentle into the night once he gets a taste of the 21st Century?"

"Goodness gracious," said McKenna. "Dylan Thomas? This from you?"

"The quote is "Do not go gentle into that good night," said Clint with a grin. "And I'm not a complete illiterate. I had an English minor in college, for heaven's sake."

"You've got a good point," said Steve. "But I don't think Oosterhuis will have a lot of choice, given what we know about your dad's illness."

"But it could be a year or more before his body gives way," said McKenna. "Therese, how much damage could he do to the business in that time?"

"I don't know," said Therese. "But I would think it would be considerable."

"Speaking of damage," said Steve. "Take a look at the eastern sky."

Far off to the south, they saw a storm rolling in with some speed, and black clouds were gathering. Steve pointed out the changing weather to the others.

"Should we retreat?" asked Therese.

"Up to you," shrugged Steve.

"No, you're the sailor," said Therese. "Tell me what you think."

Steve consulted the radar. "Well, it's going to be rough one," he said. "Like the night your father vanished. But this is a great ship and she can take it."

"Mr. Clovis?" said Therese.

"I agree with the Captain," said Clovis. "Again, though, it is up to you, Miss McNulty."

"Do we need to be afraid?" asked McKenna.

Clovis looked around the people on the bridge. "This storm does look serious," he said, indicating the sky.

"I know," said Steve. "Do you want to push ahead?"

Clovis nodded. "I am a guest, so I will not interfere," he said. "I will do whatever you wish. From what I've observed of him and his handling of the ship, I do believe Captain Blair is the equal of this storm if anyone is. "

Therese looked around at Clint and McKenna. "I think we'll be okay," she said. "What do you want to do?"

"I say we go on," said McKenna, and Clint nodded.

"Yeah," he said. "I've got a seasick patch behind my ear. I hope it works."

Steve grinned. "Maybe you should get put one behind the other ear, also," he said.

CHAPTER SEVENTEEN

The front edge of the storm struck the ship with no little violence, but, as Steve predicted, *Arcturus* rose to the challenge and handled the storm well. McKenna and Clint went to the galley, but Therese remained next to Steve on the bridge. Clovis, who had spent his life on the Cape of Good Hope, established himself at once as a skilled sailor. At Steve's suggestion, he took the wheel of *Arcturus*.

"Can we talk?" Therese said, when she and Steve were off to the side for a little while, watching the storm roll in. Funny, Therese thought, I'm not scared when I'm with him.

"I'd be pleased," Steve said. "I may be interrupted from time to time, but…"

"Have you ever heard of anything like this?" she asked.

Steve shrugged. "Legends of the *Dutchman* have been around since it foundered."

"Do you believe in the stories?" she asked.

"Well," he smiled, "I'm a sailor, so I'm pretty superstitious, as you can imagine."

"Oh, come on," she said. She smiled back at him and gave his arm a little whack.

"Miss McNulty," he began.

She interrupted. "Please," she said. "Call me Therese."

"All right," he grinned. "But I used to disregard the legends.

Still, as you know, most legends have their basis in some sort of fact. But as you also know, stories tend to get distorted as they get repeated."

Therese smiled. "When I was in high school, my Oral Communications—that is, Speech-- teacher did an exercise called 'Rumor Clinic.' He chose six people, sent five people out of the room and told a story to the one who stayed in the room. Then he called one person in, and had the first student tell the story. Then, it got repeated over and over until the last student had to tell the story to the class."

"Let me guess," said Steve, holding on to a handhold as a large waved crashed into the port side of *Arcturus*. "The story changed a little, did it?"

"You wouldn't have recognized it," she said. "What a lesson in repeating stories second and third hand."

"Yeah, what you're suggesting could have happened," said Steve. "I'm sure the stories have been embellished over the years. Still, the central idea remains. Some people even believe that the *Dutchman* wasn't destroyed. And something weird happened to us out here, I can tell you that."

"Captain?" said Clovis.

"Yes," said Steve.

"I think you should look at this."

Steve crossed to the navigation console and glanced at the radar. "Speaking of weird," he nodded. "Now, that's pretty strange." Clovis agreed.

"What is?" she said.

"I'm looking out the window at a huge front coming in," Steve frowned. "But radar isn't showing anything, Therese."

"What?" she said. She stepped next to him. The circling arm

in the radar revealed nothing but clear skies. Now she looked out the window and saw the gray, swirling mass closing on them. "But I can see…"

Steve engaged the ship to shore phone. "Coast Guard," he said. "This is *Arcturus*, San Francisco registry." He checked and gave their position. "Are you seeing a huge storm coming in?"

Silence. "Thank you," he said and signed off.

"Mr. Clovis," he barked. "Come about. Full speed to Cape Town."

The yacht turned faster than Therese expected and she lost her balance. Then she staggered backwards as the powerful engines engaged. *Arcturus* gathered speed and rocketed through the water.

Steve grabbed her and pulled her into an embrace. "Okay?" he said. Therese nodded.

"Fine," she said. Now she heard the wind outside begin pick up. "Are we going to make it?"

Steve looked grim. "I don't know," he said. "We'll try."

For an hour the *Arcturus* shot through the water, managing to stay ahead of the cloud that swirled behind them. Cape Town harbor appeared at last and *Arcturus* shot into the channel behind the breakwater, safe from the swirling clouds that seemed frustrated at not engulfing them. Clovis at last throttled back and brought the yacht into the protected breakwater.

"What was that?" gasped Therese.

"Not a clue," said Steve. He directed Clovis toward the Coast Guard Station. The tropical rainstorm struck the harbor. Rain pelted the decks of *Arcturus* and she rocked in the little swell in the safety of the harbor.

"It isn't that bad," said Clovis, looking at Steve with some surprise. "From the look of things I thought we were escaping a typhoon."

"I'm going in to the station," said Steve, his face grim. "Please help me tie us up, Mr. Clovis." The two men went out in the rain and secured the ship to the wharf.

Steve and Clovis slid out the gangway and Steve, accompanied by Therese, hastened down the walkway.

The storm continued as they hurried into the station. Steve asked to speak to the Officer of the Day.

In a few moments they were joined by a handsome, smiling officer. "I'm Commander Briton," said the man, extending his hand.

Steve introduced himself and Therese, then got to the point.

"I called for a weather report over an hour ago," he said. "The Operator told me no storm at all was on radar."

Briton frowned. He walked with Steve and Therese down to the weather center and asked for the seaman who had been on duty.

A young, handsome sailor presented himself and gave a smart salute. "Sir," he said.

Briton and the sailor chatted in Afrikaans for a few moments. "Mr. Blair," said Briton. "I don't know what to say. We have no record that you completed a call to the Coast Guard."

Steve's mouth dropped open. "What do you mean?"

"I mean, no one here took a call from you," he said.

"Could the call have been directed somewhere else?" asked Therese.

Briton turned to the young sailor. "No, sir," said the sailor. "The call would have come through here, certainly."

"Did you get a name?" asked Commander Briton. "I mean, the name of the person to whom you spoke?"

"So you believe that I called?" asked Steve.

"I believe you are a sincere man," said Briton. "I see no reason that you would make up a call to the Coast Guard."

"The sailor said his name was DeBeers," said Steve. "Seaman DeBeers."

"As in the DeBeers Cartel?" said Briton.

"Well, yes," said Steve.

"Captain Blair, we have no one here by that name," asserted Briton.

Steve turned to Therese. "What do I do?" he asked. "I have no idea."

"Let's go back to the ship," she said. "We're wasting the time of these gentlemen here."

Steve apologized to Briton, and they walked back to the boat. Steve went to the bridge. He consulted the call register. "Here it is," he said. "I show the number on call registration."

Therese nodded. "I'm certainly not calling you a liar," she said. "But how could the coast guard have no record of it?"

Clint and McKenna came onto the bridge. McKenna saw the baffled expression on Steve's face and turned to her friend. "What's happening?"

"I don't have a clue," said Therese. She explained what happened with the call, and how the Coast Guard had no idea of what they were talking about.

"They had no record of Steve's call," frowned McKenna.

"No," said Therese. "Nothing."

Clint and McKenna stared in silence. "This is just a rainstorm, not a monsoon," said Clint. "But I gather that you saw something more than the Coast Guard did on your radar. Should we have the device checked out?"

Steve shrugged. Clovis spoke up, and said he'd call a company he knew that specialized in service and care of electrical equipment. The four friends made their way to the galley, where Clovis had laid out an evening meal of cold cuts and soup.

CHAPTER EIGHTEEN

Steve opened a beer and leaned back. "I don't have a clue what to do," he said. "I can't imagine what happened."

Clint looked up. "Could it be a warning?"

McKenna did a double take. "Who would be warning us?" she asked. "What would they be warning us about?"

Clint shook his head. "Well, in all my life I've never heard of someone stealing someone's soul and replacing it with someone else's," he shrugged. "But I'm pretty sure that's what happened. Could someone force us into seeing a storm that wasn't there?"

"Look, you've lived with the Cymreig all your life," said his wife. "You know what it can do, when someone wants to change minds, or otherwise change the way a situation unfolds."

Clint thought for a moment. "Yeah, I can't deny that," he admitted. "But everyone I know who has the Cymreig wouldn't use it to…" He grew silent.

"Yes?" said Therese.

"Well, now it occurs to me," Clint said. "I've only known people who use the gift for benevolent purposes."

"And now?"

"What if someone, or even a group, uses it for mischief?"

"Mischief?" giggled McKenna.

"I didn't want to say evil," he chuckled. "But what

happened to your father, Therese, isn't good."

"From one point of view," she said.

"Is there another point of view?" he asked, surprised.

Therese shrugged. "Look at it this way," said Therese. "My father gets what he wants. He gets to live forever, and Oosterhuis gets to die in his place. He's cheated death for centuries, and now Dad gets to take his place."

"I can't quite get around on Oosterhuis, though," said McKenna. "Like your dad, he wanted to control his fate. He's willing to die in awful pain just to escape from *The Flying Dutchman*."

"Clint," said Steve. "Didn't you say that as you use the Cymreig, it gets more powerful?"

"I do notice that I'm able to do more now than I used to be able to do," he agreed. "But I try not to use the gift if I can."

"What are the limits of the Gift?" asked Steve.

"I haven't a clue," said Clint. "I haven't wanted to learn, either."

"Okay," said Therese. "Here's the next question. Could you shield the people on board so that we don't see terrifying sights?

Clint thought. "Maybe not alone," he said. "What if I'd find someone to help?

"Like who?" asked McKenna.

Clint started to reply, but Therese's cell phone buzzed. "Hello?" she said. "Mom!" she said. "Where are you?" She listened. "Okay, just a minute." She covered the mouthpiece. "You still have a rental car, don't you?" she asked McKenna, who nodded. "Can you take me to pick up my Mom?"

"Sure," said McKenna. "We parked it at the pier." She began

fishing in her purse for the keys to the rental car.

A half hour later, McKenna pulled up in front of the terminal in Cape Town. "Cape Town International is the second biggest in Africa," said her friend. "14-million passengers are expected to pass through Cape Town International By 2015."

Therese's Mom came out with a Sky Cap pushing a cart with a few small bags of luggage. Therese and her mother had an emotional greeting. "Dear one," said Mrs. McNulty. "Three years is far too long." After the Sky Cap loaded the bags into McKenna's car, Therese gave him a generous tip.

"McKenna," said Mrs. McNulty, coming over to hug McKenna. "How are you?"

McKenna gave a brief recitation of the events in her life for the last few years. Yes, Clint was fine, thanks. Right, got the doctorate six months ago. No, no children so far, but they planned to start a family soon.

"It's so wonderful of you to help us out," said Mrs. McNulty. "I appreciate you coming this far. You're a true friend to Therese."

"She's been wonderful, Mom," smiled Therese. "The best friend I've ever had."

Therese, who like her best friend McKenna stood an inch short of six feet tall, climbed into the back seat with no little difficulty, since the car was so tiny. She sat sideways with her knees scrunched against her chest. The women giggled. "Not like Dad's Lincoln when I was little," said Therese.

"Speaking of which," said Mrs. McNulty.

They stopped at a stoplight as Therese brought her mother up to date. Meanwhile McKenna looked sideways at the older woman. As usual, the woman's beauty amazed her. Mrs.

McNulty, tall and graceful, had a lovely figure. She also had—

"Mrs. McNulty," said McKenna.

"Yes, Dear," said Mrs. McNulty. "And by the way, you're a grown woman, McKenna. Can't you please call me Gayle?"

"All right," smiled McKenna. "Do you know what I mean when I use the term Cymreig?"

Silence descended on the car. Several moments went by. "Mom?" asked Therese.

"How do you know about the Cymreig?" Gayle McNulty said at last.

"My husband," said McKenna. "He has the Cymreig. He has the same red hair and green eyes that you do."

"I see," said Gayle McNulty. "I remember your husband from the wedding, but I didn't think about him having the Cymreig. Yes, of course that makes sense. I don't talk about it much, McKenna."

"No, neither does he," said McKenna.

"Mom, is this true?" asked Therese. "Do you really have the Cymreig?"

"I never wanted to tell you about it, Therese," said Gayle. "I didn't dream you'd find out. I did plan to let you know when you get married."

"Why then?" said Therese.

"Well, you might have a child, or children, who would acquire the ability," said Gayle. "It's not easy to deal with, as you may know, McKenna."

"It's true," said McKenna. "My husband's family tormented and ridiculed him, which is why he keeps it pretty much a secret. The family of my uncle Mickey treated him the same way. My mom also. She never gets in contact with her stepsisters, who hate her for the ability."

"That isn't surprising," said Gayle. "No, not at all. If you have a special talent or an ability others who know you *don't* have, you find yourself an outcast pretty much all the time."

"Is that what happened to you with Dad?" asked Therese.

"I think so," said Gayle. "He couldn't live with the idea of me knowing all his secrets."

"Did you use it on him?" asked Therese.

"I think I remember using it a few times," shrugged Gayle. "It's been quite a while, of course. If I did use it, I didn't use it often. I didn't need it. He never had much success as a liar with me, I'm afraid."

"Mom," said Therese, hesitating.

"Do you want to ask, 'What's wrong with your father?'" smiled Gayle McNulty.

"Okay, yes," said Therese.

Gayle sighed and took a deep breath. McKenna thought that she did so to keep from crying. "He called me after he talked to his Oncologist six or seven months ago," said Gayle. "Yes, a couple of months before he left on this cruise. I'm afraid it's the Big Casino, as they say in the original *Ocean's Eleven*."

"Frank Sinatra, Dean Martin, Sammy Davis Jr.?" said McKenna.

"Right," said Gayle. The little joke, McKenna realized, covered up for profound sadness and dismay. Mrs. McNulty felt a deep anguish about the pain and terror her former husband was in. McKenna thought through the anguish that Gayle must have been in, both now and when she learned that her ex-husband had contracted terminal cancer. In that moment she understood that her best friend's mother had been in pain, not to mention mortification, cause by the dreadful behavior of her friend's father.

"Gayle," said McKenna. "Do you know what's happened to Mac? Where he's gone?"

"No to both questions," said Gayle. "I know he remains in absolute terror of death, however. I remember thinking that he'd do anything to avoid dying."

"That's what I told McKenna," said Therese. "But I don't think we can comprehend such a mindset."

"His mother died, not long after we were married," said Gayle. "Her death was horrid to witness. She was not a person of faith. In fact, I'd call her antagonistic to religion. She died of cancer and the death terrified me to behold. Death dragged her out of this life in absolute trepidation, kicking and screaming in fear to almost the last moment."

"I never met her, of course," said Therese. "But it's horrible to hear such a story."

"I know, Honey, and I'm sorry," said Gayle. "I'm sorry to tell you something that awful. Believe me it was a terrible experience. But I'm certain that your father feels the same terror she did about dying. When he telephoned me about the cancer, his voice shook and he was crying tears of terror. I tried to console him, and suggested that he talk to the pastor of my church. I said that I'd make the appointment, go with him, all that—"

"He rejected it, didn't he," said Therese.

"Yes, out of hand," said Gayle. Something in her voice made McKenna turn. Gayle had tears on her cheeks. Gayle shook her head and made an effort to gain her composure. "I hope you're continuing to grow in your faith, Therese," she managed with an effort to change the conversation.

"Of course, Mom," said Therese. "But let me tell you what's happened." Therese related the story of the storm and *Arcturus*, Steve in the hospital, and Clint's encounter with Oosterhuis.

"So you think that your dad traded souls with this Oosterhuis?" asked Gayle. McKenna noticed that she didn't sound incredulous at all.

"Do you believe that's possible?" McKenna asked.

"I've seen some strange things in my life, McKenna," nodded Gayle. "Therese, I think that it's possible. I think that your father would do whatever he could to avoid the dreadful death that he was facing."

"Could he have done it without the Cymreig?" McKenna went on.

"That's quite a question, McKenna," said Gayle. She considered her answer for a few moments. "I do think it would be hard. But *The Flying Dutchman* was, of course, a ship of the Netherlands. I never heard that any of the group of Faerae lived in Holland. Remember, my ancestors fled to Ireland at the time of Norman invasion."

"My Mom's, also," said McKenna. "But if someone on the *Dutchman* has the Cymreig, wouldn't he know that they were all dead? That they were under a curse?"

"I would think so," shrugged Gayle. "And I don't know why he'd help with something like this."

A few moments later, McKenna pulled up at the dock and the three women went aboard *Arcturus*. "Greetings, Gayle," smiled Steve, extending a hand. McKenna and Clint glanced at one another. They could see that Steve liked Gayle a great deal, and she returned his affection. Clovis enjoyed his introduction to Gayle and helped her move her luggage into the master cabin.

McKenna and Therese went to the galley and helped Clovis prepare a light supper, which they served out in the wardroom. The dinner conversation was strained and difficult, as the group tried to stay positive. At last Therese asked the question that was on all of their minds.

"Look," she said. "Assume we do find the *Dutchman*. Will we know Dad? Will we then be able to bring him back?"

"Well, I have dealt with ghosts," said McKenna. "I mean, people who don't know that they're dead before. But in this case, we have a ship of people who struggle all the time with sailing a ship, living and re-living and then living again the last day of a ship. Yet somehow, they seem to have figured out that they will never again see their homes."

"What do you mean?" Steve asked.

"Well, it's like this," said Clint. "One of the things that people relate about encounters with *The Flying Dutchman* is that the crew will try to give you letters to mail to their wives and children and relatives in Holland. If you take the letters, you doom yourself to imprisonment with them. Say that's true: what if we have to send several people into eternal darkness?"

Therese shuddered. "Clint, do you mean to say that they may be better on the ship, fighting all the way until Doomsday?"

"Well, again, people without faith often live in terror of dying," Clint shrugged. "So they don't really want to go into that eternal dark."

"We've covered this," said McKenna. "Here's what I suggest. I think we should try to find the *Dutchman*, pull it out of the Cape of Good Hope channel into the Atlantic, and let the winds take care of it. I tend to think she's trapped somewhere, and we see from time to time the terror of the crew as they try to escape the fate of the Cape."'

"Wait a minute," said her husband. "Let's try to be rational. Can we help these people come to repentance and faith? After all, they are dead, aren't they?"

"I don't know that they are," said McKenna. "The legend goes on to say that the ship became sealed in time and space in a moment. It may be that they are alive, in some way that we don't understand. The men who are left, to all appearances, can't be called ghosts. They're still working as they did that day, if we understand the legends right."

"Can they find salvation in the time it takes for us to tow the *Dutchman* out of these seas?" asked Therese.

"That's what I mean," said Clint.

"McKenna," said Mrs. McNulty. "The stories we see on television suggest that ghosts are uniform in their malevolence, seeking to destroy and kill. Is that your experience?"

"No, it isn't," said McKenna. "Ghosts, by definition, are people who can't let life go. They had something they had to maintain, to solve, to find, things like that. In one case, I met a couple who devoted their lives to finding the treasure of Blackbeard. In a disastrous irony, they died in a car accident when they crashed into the side of an ice wagon. They refused to let their lives go and kept re-living the hunt for the treasure."

"I imagine what you're saying is true," said Mrs. McNulty.

"Then on White Island we encountered the ghost of a young woman named Martha Herring," said McKenna. "She died in 1735 and stayed to guard the treasure of her pirate husband

Sandy Gordon. What a creep he was."

"But Martha was good, and sweet, and she married an ancestor of yours, didn't she?" said Clint.

"Right," said McKenna. "She saved him from slavery in 1720 or so."

"So you've never encountered a malevolent spirit, is that right?" asked Gayle McNulty.

"Yes," said McKenna. "That has been my experience. But Clint, you think this Oosterhuis is evil, right?

"I tend to think that someone who could create that storm image in our minds yesterday has power beyond anything we can imagine, at least," Clint acquiesced. "On the other hand, someone who would use the Cymreig merely to frighten people would have to be called Evil, yes. Remember, the Coast Guard saw a rainstorm, not a storm of epic proportions."

"You mean you think that someone wanted to warn us off?" asked Steve.

"Here's something else," said Gayle. "Can you and I shield the people on the ship from this person? Or, now that I think about it, it could be more than one individual, right?"

"Also for *that* matter, what do we see as the endgame in this?" asked Steve. "We plan to go out to save a man who treated me like trash, who didn't value my opinion or expertise, who's entered into this floating terror on purpose. I'm sorry, Therese, I love you, but I'm not altogether crazy about fighting the Cape anymore."

"What did you say?" Therese asked.

"I said, I don't want to fight the storms on the Cape anymore," said Steve. "Going around the Horn in any weather—"

"No, no, I got that," she said. "Before that."

"Oh," he said. "I said, 'I love you.'"

"I thought so," she said. "The thing is, I'm afraid I love you, too."

"Oh," said Steve again. Therese got up, crossed the cabin to him, and they began to kiss.

Gayle, McKenna and Clint watched for a few moments.

"McKenna," said Gayle.

"Yes?" she answered.

"Did you know how they felt about each other?" murmured Gayle.

"Well, Therese told me," said McKenna. "But I didn't quite get it with Steve, so, well…" Her voice trailed off.

Clint and McKenna laughed and Gayle smiled. They left the room in silence.

Chapter Nineteen

The next day dawned bright, warm and pleasant. McKenna and Clint sat on the aft deck of *Arcturus* with a cup of coffee and the Cape Town newspapers, enjoying the lovely weather.

Therese, looking bright and glowing, came onto the deck with a cup of coffee. She sat down with Clint and McKenna and exchanged greetings.

Silence descended for a while. At last Therese asked, "Reading the paper?"

"Yes," said McKenna, trying not to laugh at her old friend. "*The*—uh—*Daily Dispatch*."

"Yeah," said Clint, not able to meet his wife's eyes for fear of laughing in Therese's face. "Good paper."

"Uh, huh," said Therese.

"Want some of it?" asked Clint.

"No thank you," said Therese. Silence descended.

"Well?" said McKenna.

"Well what?" asked Therese, looking innocent.

"Oh, come on," said McKenna. "You look like you could light up Cape Town."

Therese smiled. "Okay," she said. "We're getting married."

McKenna's jaw dropped. "What!" she cried. Clint laughed and offered congratulations as his wife embraced her friend.

"Yes," said Therese, blushing. "We talked it over after you

all went to bed. We decided that we'd had enough of not being together."

"But isn't this kind of sudden?" asked McKenna.

"No," said Therese. "I've known him for years. Dad's had him on the yacht for ten years."

"Ah," said Clint. "And you're the reason he hasn't quit, I imagine."

Therese grinned and the blush even more intense. "Well, he agreed to help me look for Dad," she said. "And no, I didn't make that a condition of agreeing to marry him."

McKenna laughed. Clint hugged Therese in congratulation. "I didn't ask that," said Clint.

Gayle came up the ladder carrying a cup of coffee. She was beaming also.

"Therese told you," said McKenna.

"Yes," nodded Gayle. "I couldn't be more pleased. Steve's a fine man."

Mother and daughter hugged for a few moments. Conversation revolved around the wedding and some preliminary plans.

"Speaking of plans," said Gayle. "Have we an idea of how we're going to proceed now?"

Clint started to answer, but at that moment Steve came on deck. He didn't appear to be as cheerful as usual, the others noted. Clint and Gayle exchanged looks.

"Has something happened, Steve?" asked Gayle.

"I just got a call from the hospital," said Steve. "I'm afraid that Oosterhuis isn't doing at all well."

Silence descended. "Do they know how much time he has?" asked Gayle.

Steve shrugged. "They don't think he'll last much longer,"

he said, "Though of course they can't predict. I guess I didn't realize things were that serious. If we want to question him, we should do it soon."

* * * * *

The group went to the Groote Schuur Hospital, where they found Oosterhuis with oxygen tubes under his nose. His eyes, which had been fanatical and evil, were relaxed and calm, and his jaw was set with determination. "This is your father," nodded one of the nurses.

"Yes," said Therese.

"And my ex-husband," said Gayle.

The nurse nodded. "You can stay with him," she said. "He can't last too much longer. He's asked us to discontinue all intervention except pain medication."

Therese and Gayle nodded. Clint touched Gayle's elbow and they went together into the hallway.

"Are you surprised by this turn of events?" said Clint.

"No," said Gayle, shaking her head. "I'm sure that Oosterhuis is anxious to die and has surrendered to that eventuality."

"What happens to his body?" asked Clint. "Can we keep it alive until we find McNulty?"

Gayle shrugged. "Can the body survive without a soul?" she asked. "I don't know. I don't think so."

"Okay," said Clint. "Then does it make sense for us to continue the quest for the *Dutchman*? Should we let McNulty have his way?"

"I just don't know how to answer that," said Gayle. "It seems to me that if you can save a life, you ought to. But in this case, Mac's body will expire in moments and Oosterhuis' soul will go to wherever judgment sends him."

"What should we do?"

"Have you Paiked Oosterhuis?"

"Yes," said Clint.

"Why don't we both go in and see if we can learn where *The Flying Dutchman* is?"

Clint shuddered at the thought of going back into the soul of the man. He thought it over. "I guess we could do that," he said. "At any case we can try to ease his mind, perhaps his soul?" Gayle agreed.

They returned to the room. "What's up, Clint?" asked McKenna.

"We're going to try something," said Clint. "I don't know what will happen."

Gayle took the hand of the man on the bed, one which had once been hers. Clint laid his hand on McNulty's arm. They looked at each other, and then at McNulty's eyes. The room vanished in swirls of color and lights and then resolved itself. They found themselves on a sailing ship.

"Where are we?" Gayle asked. They stood under a grey, forbidding sky. They saw blood red sails on the masts, and ropes and rigging were taut with tension.

"We're on the *Dutchman*," said Clint. "Not really, of course, but this is where Oosterhuis lives. I imagine he will stay in this place forever, for all eternity."

"What do you mean?" said a snarling voice just behind them.

"You escaped this place," said Clint. "But this is still who you are, Oosterhuis. I'm afraid you're going to spend all eternity here, aboard *the Flying Dutchman*, trying to round the Cape of Good Hope."

"No!" screamed Oosterhuis. No one on the ship paid him any attention. He ran to one of the men. "Roggens!" he shrieked. He tried to grab the man's arm, but he couldn't gain a grip. Nor did the man seem to hear him at all. Oosterhuis tried another man, with the same result. And another.

Oosterhuis turned back to Gayle and Clint.

"What can I do?" he asked.

"We can help you pray, if you wish," said Clint.

"Yes," said Gayle. "But you have to do it now."

"But I'll still have to live here, won't I," asked Oosterhuis.

"I think you still have a choice," said Clint. "You are still alive. Though not for long."

"Very well," said Oosterhuis. "Can you help me?"

Clint and Gayle put their hands on Oosterhuis' shoulder. Clint led Oosterhuis through a simple prayer of commitment, asking God for forgiveness of all his sins and praying for Him to save him from eternal punishment. Oosterhuis said the prayers, devoutly and sincerely.

Now his features began to change. Clint and Gayle saw a radiance begin to surround him.

"Clint, he only has a few seconds," said Gayle. "We have to go now."

"Yes," said Clint. "One question. Oosterhuis. Where is this?"

"I think we're frozen in ice," said the sailor. "The crew doesn't know it."

"Can we help?" said Gayle. Now, a set of huge black gates stood open behind him.

"You have already helped me," said Oosterhuis, and the first smile either Gayle or Clint had seen on him played across his features. The sneer, the frown of contempt, the ugly twisting that had characterized the man's countenance relaxed. He smiled at the two people who had come with him to stand at the Black Gates. "Thank you. I see what you mean. I am at peace, please believe me." He turned and walked with confidence through the gates.

The ship had begun melting away. "Clint!" screamed Gayle. "Now!"

Clint slid backwards from the man's mind and staggered as the hospital room appeared around him. "Gayle!" he cried.

"I'm here!" she asserted, but her voice trembled with fear. "I have never come that close to death before."

Clint nodded. "I agree," he gave a soft grin. "It appears we made it back." McKenna and Therese were hugging them now and Clint turned to look at the bed. A body lay on the bed, still and unmoving. Clint, who had seen death before, thought he saw the remains of a slight smile.

Now he became aware of the persistent tone from the monitors above the bed. A nurse entered the room and checked Oosterhuis' body. She reached up and turned off the respirator and the tone faded.

"Are you all right?" asked McKenna with tears of worry in her eyes. He realized that she was afraid that he'd gone too close to death.

Clint smiled and squeezed her hand in reassurance. "Yeah, I'm fine, Honey," he said and gave her a look of profound comfort and love. Then he leaned to his wife, took her in his arms and gave her a long kiss. He didn't want to let go.

"Ahem," said Therese. "Clint! Mickey!"

The married couple backed out of the kiss. "Yeow," said McKenna.

"I'm sorry," said Clint, wiping tears from his check.

"Sorry for what?" smiled McKenna. "You just made my day, Buster." She hugged him and stroked the tears on his face away.

"Well, I can't pass up an opportunity like that," said Steve, and he kissed Therese.

"Oh, good grief," said Gayle. "Come on, let's go back to the boat."

"I think that's a terrific idea," said Therese.

Before they could go back to *Arcturus*, however, they had some paperwork to take care of with the hospital. The question arose what should they do with McNulty's body. "Well, his will is on the ship," said Therese.

"I know what he wanted," said Steve. "He told me a few nights ago. He wanted his body cremated and the ashes scattered on the ocean. It's in his will."

"That's okay," said Gayle.

"Wait a minute," said Clint. "I thought—please forgive me for this—that Mac would have a woman with him for this trip."

"He did," said Steve with a wry smile. "When he almost died, she asked for a ride to the airport in Cape Town."

"True loyalty," said McKenna.

"Something like that," said Therese.

Gayle stood in silence as the orderlies took the body out of the room. McKenna exchanged a look with Clint. Then she crossed to her. "Gayle?" she whispered.

Gayle turned, tears of grief and pain on her cheek. She wiped at her eyes. "I didn't expect to see him die," she said, and her tears began to flow.

"Now what?" asked Clint.

"I guess we have a funeral at sea tomorrow," said Gayle. "If all of you could possibly help out with and take part in it, I'd appreciate it."

"Of course," said McKenna. "We'd be honored." The others agreed with her.

Gayle began to weep again, a quiet fall of tears, as her daughter embraced her. "Oh," she said to Clint. "That isn't quite what you meant, is it?"

"Well, no," he said. "As I think about it, I asked an inappropriate question. Please accept my apologies."

Gayle waved her hand in dismissal. "No," she said. "You have nothing to apologize for. You're here at some expense, away from home, doing us a favor. Of course it wasn't inappropriate." She took Clint's hand and then leaned up to give him a brief hug.

She sighed. "I guess I have to let a bunch of people know, don't I?"

"I can take care of a lot of that, Mom," said Therese. "But let's not worry about that tonight, or even for a few days. I'll have the office handle a lot of the contacts and detail. You just relax."

"I guess," said Gayle.

"Things will probably look different after a night's sleep," put in McKenna. "I think you're right, Therese."

"What happened when you Paiked Oosterhuis?" asked Therese.

Clint and Gayle talked about finding themselves on the *Dutchman*, surrounded by crewman, all of whom were unaware of them. "I think that's what scared Oosterhuis the most," said Gayle.

"Yes," confirmed Clint. "He saw himself in a unique vision of Hell."

"How's that?" asked his wife.

"One major statement about Hell," said Clint. "Many people say that it involves utter separation from God. Remember Romeo's cry of agony? 'Banished! That is the cry of the damned in Hell!'"

"Right," said McKenna. "And Oosterhuis saw what his future—his eternity—would be like, you think?" Gayle and Clint agreed.

"Then, however, he said a brief prayer of commitment," said Gayle. "The vision changed and he saw new possibilities for eternity. Certainly that vision didn't include *The Flying Dutchman*. We couldn't see what he saw, but we did see the terror disappear."

"Very moving," said Clint. "I mean it. I watched him walk through the gates of heaven, I think."

"You didn't see Dad, I guess," said Therese. Then she realized. "Of course, you wouldn't know him anyway."

"I tried to sense him," said Gayle. "But we were very focused on helping Oosterhuis save his soul. And we barely made it back, you know," she concluded.

"Okay, then, should we go to find the *Dutchman*?" said Clint. "If that's possible."

"I think it is," said Gayle. "I had the sense that we weren't moving, that the wind wasn't in the sails."

"You know, you're right," said Clint. "Yeah, I sensed we were on the *Dutchman*, but that nothing at all was happening. Everything seemed to be frozen in time, or in ice, or something."

"Were the crewmen alive?" asked Steve.

"I don't know," said Clint, and Gayle nodded.

"I felt that we were watching a museum display of a ship,"

she said. "The sails were rigged, the ropes were taut, and the activity on the ship seemed to be normal. I think."

"But something just felt wrong," said Clint. "I thought we were inside a dream. I mean, it felt like what Oosterhuis showed us was not the way things are." Gayle nodded.

"I agree," she said. "It was like we were watching—what?—a living haunted house from Halloween."

The group fell silent. "Do you have any idea where it is?" asked McKenna after a few moments.

"Not offhand," said Clint. "I think we could Paik one another and get some ideas from one another's perception."

"Cold," said Gayle. "Very cold. Like in a refrigerator."

"Yes," said Clint. "I wasn't comfortable, that's for sure."

"Remember what Stephen King says?" said McKenna. "In his book *The Stand*, one of the characters says to another, 'When you get to Hell, you'll find it's cold.'"

"So were you in Hell?" said Steve, speaking up for the first time in a while. Clint and Gayle exchanged glances and nodded. "Weren't you terrified?" He asked.

"No, not exactly," said Gayle.

"I agree," said Clint. "We were focused on finding out information, we knew we weren't dead, and besides, we didn't see our picture of hell. We witnessed him in his: all alone, no contacts, no changes ever."

"All the same, we experienced his terror," said Gayle. "He saw what was waiting for him."

"Yeah, we could feel how scared he was," nodded Clint.

"Is that what's waiting for Dad?" asked Therese, her voice small and scared.

"I don't know," said Gayle. "I think we need to find him and try to make sure it isn't."

"We'll help, Therese and Gayle," said McKenna. "Clint and me, we're with you."

"No," said Gayle as Therese shook her head. "You've done more than enough. Yes, you have. I want you to get on an airplane and go home."

"Absolutely correct," said Therese. "You've been true friends and I don't want to endanger you anymore."

"You too, Steve," began Gayle.

"Not a chance," said Steve. "I've waited my whole life to meet the woman I'm going to spend my life with. Now I'm married to her—"

"What!" said McKenna.

"Yes," said Therese. "We got married in Cape Town this morning."

"Ohmigosh," moaned Gayle, hugging her daughter in congratulation. "And I wanted you to have a beautiful wedding—"

"I had it, Mom," grinned Therese.

"No kidding," said Steve. "The best of all time."

"But your honeymoon," said Gayle.

"I'm married to the man I love, living on the boat, on an adventure looking for a legend, hoping to save my father and many others. What could be better than that?" asked Therese.

"Well," smiled Steve. "Offhand, I can think of one thing."

"Sex maniac," laughed McKenna.

"I tell you what," said Therese. "What if we have a big wedding and a reception when we conclude this quest?"

Gayle smiled. "Perfect," she said.

CHAPTER TWENTY

The next day *Arcturus* set out heading south. A storm seemed a remote possibility today: the sky was blue, cloudless, and bright with the African sun. "Couldn't ask for much better sailing weather," noted Clint.

Steve nodded. The two men stood on the bridge of *Arcturus*, coffee cups in hand, looking out at the horizon.

"Congratulations again," said Clint.

"Yeah, thanks," said Steve. "You know, I love the sea, and sailing. I've had some great thrills, adventures. But without going into detail, nothing will ever beat last night in my life."

Clint grinned at his friend. "When do we reach position?"

Steve shrugged. "Pretty soon. Are you and Gayle set?"

"I hope so," said Clint.

McKenna, also carrying coffee, came up onto the bridge. She greeted the two men.

"How can the rest of us help?" she asked.

"I don't know," said Clint. "I've never tried something like this. It's like I'm communicating across time and space."

McKenna nodded. "We'll stay right next to you."

Now Gayle entered the bridge. She embraced Steve and kissed his cheek. "Good morning, Son," she giggled.

"I think it's a shame," noted McKenna, "that you can't seem to work up any enthusiasm for this marriage, Gayle." The rest of their friends on the bridge chuckled.

"Yes, I am thrilled," said Gayle. "Therese couldn't have married a finer man."

Clovis came up on deck and gestured to Clint. "Gayle," said Clint. He motioned to her and they walked out onto the deck, where Clovis started talking to them with a great deal of animation.

"Where's Therese?" asked McKenna.

"I told her to sleep in for a while," Steve replied. "This could be a full day."

McKenna shrugged. "Yes, maybe," she agreed. "Can I get you some coffee?"

"Thanks, yes," he said. "I'm nodding a little myself. Not much sleep last night."

McKenna giggled. "The weather's gorgeous, isn't it?" she said. "Beautiful for sailing." Then, looking to the southeast, she noted, "That's the only cloud in the sky."

Steve nodded and glanced at the cloud. "Kind of a funny color for a day like this," he said.

McKenna looked back. "Yeah," she mused.

The tension level went up. Clint and Gayle came back into the cabin. "They're coming," he said. "Mr. Clovis sensed them." Clovis stood at the railing, staring in obvious fear at the black cloud.

McKenna stared for a second. "Who's coming?"

Clint pointed to the cloud. "The wind's out of the north," he said. "That cloud's moving into the wind from the south."

"Do you sense anything?" said Gayle.

Clint shook his head. "Nothing," he told them. "But then I didn't sense anything the last time we saw a cloud either."

"I don't know," said Gayle. "I'm feeling some real discomfort on the other hand. It's getting more powerful as that cloud approaches."

Clint turned and looked at the cloud. Now, he heard a whisper. A voice seemed to be speaking to him, but words were inaudible. "Who could that be?"

Gayle shrugged. "I don't know either," she said.

"Steve," said Clint. "Take us toward that cloud. Something is going on, I don't know what."

Steve looked up and saw Therese enter the bridge also. "Therese," he said. "Look, we want to explore that cloud. It's your ship. What do you say?"

Therese turned to Clint and her mother. "Do you think we'll be heading into danger?" she asked.

"We don't know, either one of us," said Gayle and Steve nodded agreement.

"Yeah, okay," he said. *Arcturus* turned and headed directly toward the cloud.

Within a few moments, the voice began to clarify in Clint's mind. "Stay away," it said. "You are entering into a world you cannot imagine."

"Did you hear that?" he asked Gayle. She nodded.

"It's getting clearer," she agreed. "I don't recognize the voice."

"What do you mean?" he blinked.

"I thought it might be Mac."

* * * * *

Mac McNulty understood, somehow, that he had come aboard a dead ship. He'd been in the yacht Arcturus when he saw a man climb aboard, and walk in a straight line toward him.

"Who are you?" he demanded in his best Mac McNulty voice, the one before which strong men had been cowed. "What do you want?"

"My name is Oosterhuis," said the man. "I'm here to make you an offer."

"Me?" said McNulty. "You want to offer me something? What on earth could you offer me?"

"You're about to die," said Oosterhuis. "I can fix it so you won't, not ever."

"What!" said Mac.

The man nodded. "I know that Death has his hand on you," he said. "You haven't much time. Only a few more days. You'll have to go ashore into a hospital very soon, isn't that right?"

"Yes," Mac said. McNulty felt the terror building, as it always did when he considered his own mortality. He began to cry, something few people had ever seen. "Yes," he said. "I'm afraid of Hell for my sins, also."

"There may be worse things than Hell," said the man. Now Mac felt at home. He stood on the bridge of his mighty yacht, talking business with a business man, and he dealt with businessmen all the time. He'd made a fortune by his ability to sense what the other man was thinking, what the bottom line was, and how it could benefit him.

He looked around and saw his bridge crew trying to speak, but unable to move or communicate, their eyes filled with terror. "Go on," he said.

Oosterhuis smiled. "The rest of my ship is frozen in time, at this minute," he said. "I'm here on very borrowed time. You have to accept or decline right now. Will you trade bodies with me?"

"Yes, but…" said McNulty---

--And then he found himself on a sailing ship, frozen in time.

He stood and looked around him. The men were dressed in strange costumes—knee britches, wool coats, high socks and buckled shoes. A man approached.

The man swung a weapon at him. It was a type of whip, with several leather thongs, and metal balls tied to the thongs. It hurt like the devil when it hit him.

"What the hell is that?" he asked, ready to strike back.

"Get back down there and scrub," said the man. He turned to go, but McNulty yelled at him.

"Who are you?" said Mac. The man didn't answer. He swung the vicious whip with all his strength.

Mac was ready this time. He stepped inside the blow and seized the whip. He jerked it out of the hand of the shocked man and threw it over the side.

"I asked you a question," Mac said. "I asked, 'who are you.'"

The man drew a pistol. He leveled it at McNulty. "You're looking at two dozen right now, Oosterhuis," he said. "Don't make it worse." He made a gesture.

"Two dozen what?" said McNulty. Then his arms were pinioned behind him. Two men dragged him to a rack. Two other men stripped away Mac's coat and then his shirt. He almost screamed in the cold air.

Before he quite knew what was happening, the mate had produced another cat with small bits of bone tied to the thongs. The man knew what he was doing. McNulty passed out at the twelfth lashing. He came to when a crewman sluiced his back with a bucket of ice water.

Two men cut the leather thongs binding him to the rack. Mac McNulty fell backward to the deck and banged his head hard on the oak deck. The impact of his back smashing onto the deck made him scream with pain.

"Get him below," sneered the mate. The two men took his shoulders and dragged him toward a hatch.

"Avast, you men," yelled a voice. The two men dragging McNulty dropped his arms and stood at attention.

"Captain," the mate yelled back.

"We're going through," yelled the Captain.

No looks were exchanged. They could feel the ship plunging, heeling, straining against the wind, coming alee from a starboard tack. "Sir," yelled the mate with a salute. He began bellowing commands.

The crew leapt into action. While they labored with the sails and the ropes, McNulty saw the captain spring into the netted ropes and begin to ascend to the Crow's Nest. McNulty realized what he was about to do. "No!" he screamed. "We'll be trapped here forever!"

The mate turned and pointed. One of the men who'd been dragging McNulty smashed his fist into McNulty's face and everything went black again.

* * * * *

Mac woke up in a bunk as someone yelled a wake-up call. He moved with some care, worried that his back would be too sore…

But it didn't hurt at all. Not in the slightest.

He felt at his nose. No pain. No bruising on his face.

"Get up and onto deck, Oosterhuis," screamed the mate. "This storm has grown worse!"

McNulty pulled on some clothes, bewildered. He went up on deck and a mate gestured to a rope. "Get to work!" yelled the mate.

All of this seemed familiar. He recognized conversations that he'd heard yesterday. He knelt onto the deck and took a brush from a bucket nearby. He began to scrub. Someone splashed soapy water onto the deck and he scrubbed. And scrubbed.

Once he slowed down and leaned up to stretch his back. The taskmaster rewarded him with the lash of a cane across his shoulders. The mate didn't speak when he did it. He moved on to whack the next slacker.

At that point, he got it. This was his life. This was what he would do for the rest of eternity: scrubbing the same square of decking. He'd experience the same day, the same storm, and the same lashings if he spoke up. The same day, lived over and over, ending when the captain ascended to the top of the main mast and yelled curses at heaven. The same chores. Scrubbing the same section of the same deck again and again and again.

He didn't get a beating again that day. Nor the next. A plan began to form, though.

* * * * *

The *Arcturus* didn't flee today. "No," said Clint. "Face the ship into the storm. Go right at it."

"What!" said Steve.

"I agree with Clint, Steve," said Gayle. "We need to confront this situation. I don't believe it's a real storm."

"Not a real storm?" gasped Steve.

"I see what they're saying," said McKenna. "I think someone is playing with our minds."

Steve frowned. He picked up the satellite phone and called

the South African Coast Guard. He connected to Commander Briton. "Commander," he said. "Are you tracking a storm fifteen miles or so south from Cape Town?" He listened in silence. "Thank you, Commander," he said, and hung up, looking bewildered.

"Well?" said Therese. Steve chewed at his lip.

"They see nothing," he said. "They're seeing a cloudless day, one of the nicest on record off the Cape."

"I thought so," said Clint, and Gayle agreed.

"I think someone is messing with our minds," said Clint. "I don't know how, but whoever it or they are, they're doing something beyond our ability. Certainly mine."

"Mine too," agreed Gayle.

"Can we defend ourselves?" asked Therese.

Gayle and Clint shrugged. *They aren't afraid at all,* thought Therese. *Neither is McKenna. How do they manage that?*

Arcturus slowed to about 15 knots as they reached the cloud. The waves now became gigantic, and the wind howled at gale strength. "Actual wind speed?" asked Therese.

"We're not tracking it," said Steve, still looking bewildered.

"No," said Clint. "This is an illusion."

Now the cloud seemed to move and enveloped the yacht in near darkness.

"Don't be scared," said Gayle. "This is not happening." *Arcturus* continued creeping forward. Several minutes passed. And then...

"What happened?" asked McKenna. "It's perfectly calm."

"Right," said Clint. "It has been."

Now, the ocean ahead of them appeared calm and quiet. "Has it always been like this?" asked Steve.

"Just like this," said Clint.

"Something is going to happen, though," nodded Gayle. "Again, don't let the fear get you."

Now the sea beside them boiled and stirred. As they watched, a monstrous shape rose with slow, terrible determination.

"What is it?" asked Therese, grasping Steve's elbow.

"I think we're being shown Kraken," he said. "In all its terrible glory."

Now the sea around them erupted and monstrous tentacles broke the water. A gigantic shape, resembling an octopus, menaced them. A tentacle encircled the yacht, while another reached for a crewman and seized him.

The crewman screamed in terror. The tentacle lifted him off the deck and pulled him toward a clacking, horrid beak almost like that of a gigantic bird. Steve screamed "Langley! No!" He reached for a rifle and started toward a window.

"No," yelled Clint. "Let me help." He took Steve's arms and looked into his eyes. In a moment Steve calmed down and the sea resumed its gentle swell.

"What about Langley?" he asked. Then his eyes cleared. "We have no one on board named Langley," he said. "Is this all a dream?"

"Yes," said Gayle, and embraced Therese, who trembled with fear. "Well, not quite a dream. An illusion, brought on by someone."

"Who would do that?" asked McKenna.

"Who even could do that?" responded Therese. "Or who would want to?"

Clint shrugged. "I'd say it's someone who doesn't want us to move ahead."

Now a dark cave appeared before them. The entrance to the cave appeared to be surrounded by fire.

"Same thing," said Gayle. "An illusion. Full speed ahead."

The *Arcturus* appeared to plunge over a waterfall as it entered the cave. The people on the bridge gritted their teeth…

Then, the ocean grew calm, the sky became clear and *Arcturus* was making 10 knots through the waters off the Cape of Good Hope.

"What happened?" asked Therese.

"The Cymreig," said Gayle. "Someone has the Gift but doesn't want us to approach."

"Approach what?" asked Therese.

"I think they want us to stay away from the vessel," said Clint. "*The Flying Dutchman,* I mean."

"They?" asked McKenna. "Is there more than one?"

"Could be," said Clint. "If it's only one, it's the strongest manifestation of the Cymreig I've ever seen."

"Can you guys communicate with them?" McKenna asked.

"I don't have any sense of welcome for that," said Clint.

Gayle agreed. "This person appears to be angry, frustrated, and maybe even wicked," she said.

"Shall we go on?" asked Steve.

"I think so," said Clint. "We seem to be able to sense the use of the Gift and so far we've been able to neutralize it."

"This is terrifying," said McKenna.

"Hell *is* terrifying," said Gayle.

The decision to proceed sobered the group. "Let's talk it over a bit," suggested Therese. Steve nodded and throttled back the huge yacht's engines.

"What's our goal in this?" asked McKenna.

"I thought we were clear, Mickey," said her friend. "We want to rescue my dad from a horrible decision."

"I see where Mickey's going," said Steve. "Look, he's an adult. He can make his own decisions, can't he?"

Therese got mad. "Look, this is easy for you guys to say," she snapped. "It's not your father who's damned for all eternity."

"I don't have parents," said Clint. "They threw me out years ago."

"The man who I thought was my father is in prison for the next several years," McKenna added. "It's a complicated story, you know, but it was hell for a while, what he put me through."

"But you've been united with your real father," said Therese.

"The point is, we've been through a lot with our parents," said McKenna. "You're not the only one."

Therese began to cry. Steve put his arm around her and embraced her shoulders. "Of course I'm going to stand with you, Therese. So are your friends. But what we're saying—well, I'm saying it, I can't speak for these guys, of course—is this: say we find the *Dutchman*. Say we're in a position to rescue your dad. Would we be doing the right thing?"

"How do we know?" asked Therese. "No one ever gets told what will happen. We get options presented to us. We try to make the best decision we can."

Gayle nodded. "This is going to sound strange, I'm afraid," she said. "But I think I know him better than anyone here. Mac has spent his life making decisions. Business decisions presented no difficulty because he only thought about himself. If he thought something would benefit him, he'd do it. If he thought something would make him happy, he'd do it, without reference to other people's feelings, concerns, or wishes."

"Is that what happened here?" asked Steve.

"Probably," said Gayle. "He knew he was going to die, soon and hard. So he forced you, Steve, to drive the boat through the storm. If the ship went down, he'd die in short order, drowned in the ocean off the Cape of Good Hope. As terrible as it sounds, drowning would beat dying the lingering and horrible, pain-ridden death he had staring him in the face."

"So he'd be willing to live on the ghost ship, reliving the same day, day after day, year after year, by choice?" said McKenna.

Gayle nodded. "You don't understand him," she said. "I know he sees it as an organization. It has a structure and a discipline enforced by fear. He's used to that. He always ran all his companies that way: go in, fire as many people as you have to, bring in your own men, and terrify everyone left from the previous group."

"Did it work?" asked Steve.

"It didn't matter," Gayle shrugged. "I imagine he's seeing the treasure now. He'll take command of the ship if he can."

"But Dad doesn't know anything about sailing," said Therese. "The Master of a ship has to know every aspect of the vessel, right?"

"It never stopped him before," Gayle said. "He never knew anything about the businesses he took over. He'd learn as he went along." Therese nodded.

Arcturus plowed ahead through moderate seas and no more visions showed up. At lunch, Therese asked Gayle, "Why do you think the dreams stopped?"

Gayle considered. "I've been thinking about that. Frankly I

don't have a clue. The only guess I can make is that somehow the person—or people, it could be more than one—sensed me and Clint. As Clint said, I have met people who have the Gift—"

"The Cymreig?" asked McKenna.

Gayle nodded. "But I've never met someone who was evil, or who used the Gift for evil," she said. "To those of us who have it—at least, those I've met—misuse would be almost unthinkable."

"Can you tell us more about the Cymreig?"

"Not much," she said. "I know about our direct ancestor, whose name was Viviane."

"When was this?" asked McKenna.

"No one knows the exact date," said Gayle. "Probably the sixth or seventh century. Once in a while, the gift will emerge in a person with far more intensity than in others. Your mother and Clint and I are by no means as powerful as they are."

"Was this in England?" asked Therese.

"First England, then Ireland and to all appearances, Holland as well."

"England?" said McKenna. "Are you talking about Myrthynne and the Crystal Cave?"

Therese looked at her in surprise. "Are you saying Merlin? As in King Arthur?"

"Well, yes," said McKenna. "His real name has been altered over the centuries to, as you say, Merlin."

"Have you been to the Crystal Cave?" asked Gayle.

"Yes," said McKenna. "Myrthynne brought me."

"Tell me the story," said Therese. McKenna nodded and began to relate the legend her mother had told her.

French and Viking mercenaries lurked in the woods all around Myrthynne. Mordred, the king's bastard son, had charged them to hunt down Myrthynne and his apprentice and kill them. The mercenaries, however, lived in terror of him. They yet lacked the courage to attack.

Myrthynne could use the Cymreig to confuse most of them, but Nehushtan could shield a few of them long enough to set upon him.

Nehushtan had won, at least this time. The battle, however, wouldn't cease as long as the Cymreig existed. Viviane and Myrthynne could confuse the mercenaries enough so that she could escape with Gareth, the young Welsh knight, who had come to live with them.

Gareth would defend them to the death. *No*, thought Myrthynne. *Gareth must not be in danger for me.*

Tears of despair and pain welled in Myrthynne's eyes. He looked over at his adopted daughter, realizing he would never see Viviane again.

Myrthynne wanted to welcome and enjoy the children who would come when she married Gareth. Myrthynne cherished Viviane like a daughter. The nineteen-year-old had grown into a true beauty, with copper colored hair, emerald eyes, and a lithe figure.

Myrthynne sighed. He knew he'd miss her as much as he'd miss the king, his best friend and former student. At least Myrthynne would see Arthur again, when Time came full circle.

Until that time, Myrthynne had to seal himself in his cave, where time and space weren't quite the same as they were elsewhere. With Viviane's help, he could cast deep doubt in the minds of the mercenaries charged to hunt him down and kill him. She and Gareth could still escape.

Viviane, like Myrthynne, had inherited the Cymreig. Myrthynne, though, would become the most famous person ever born with the ability as well as the most powerful. A form of his name would someday turn out to be synonymous with magic and sorcery.

The legends of Myrthynne would say that a young woman betrayed him. In a moment of weakness he revealed the secret of the Cymreig. The world would remember her as a whore or a witch who enchanted him into a Crystal Cave or an oak tree to live a wretched existence of imprisonment, neither dead nor alive.

But Viviane—whom the legends would also name Nimue, Vivienne, and several other names--didn't betray him. She loved Myrthynne as she would her father.

Myrthynne first saw Viviane, a terrified ten-year-old orphan, begging food to survive. Myrthynne rode with Arthur into a village that had been devastated by a gang of bandits.

The king and his knights had caught all but a few of the thieves. Bedivere, Bors, Lionel and a few others were still in pursuit of those who had escaped. Those who had been apprehended were dangling from trees outside the village or lying beheaded in a ditch.

The other knights began distributing food and clothing to the desperate villagers. Several would stay to help the villagers rebuild.

Myrthynne first saw her standing by the road at the end of the village. The girl looked up at him. When he saw her emerald eyes peering through disheveled, filthy copper-colored hair, he sensed the Cymreig within the child.

He dismounted and walked to her. She drew back, frightened.

"Don't be afraid, precious one," he said. He took her hand and she relaxed a little. He looked into her green eyes. "Be at peace. Tell me your name."

"Viviane," she murmured.

"Be still, and look in my eyes, Viviane," he told her. She obeyed.

He Paiked the secret places in her mind. He felt her astonishment to meet someone who had the ability to do what she could do. She Paiked back.

The sorcerer showed her that an unseen enemy known as Nehushtan or the Snake posed a mortal danger. She had sensed the peril all her life. But she knew she faced no danger from Myrthynne.

As they dropped the mental link she managed a weak smile. He knelt before her and took her in his arms.

Her shaky veneer of strength slipped away. She hugged him back. He felt her sobs of grief and terror against his shoulder.

"What happened to your parents?" he asked so only she could hear him.

"Dead," said the child, voice quavering. She pointed to the burned and charred remains of a small hut. "The bad men killed them last week."

Myrthynne knew why the bandits murdered her parents. Nehushtan.

The child's lip trembled with grief. "No one took you in,

Beloved?" Myrthynne asked. "Or fed you?"

"No, sir," said the child through her tears. "They fear me. They call me a witch."

The sorcerer stood, and regarded the villagers who were standing nearby. He struggled not to lash out in fury at the people of the village.

The villagers knew the great sorcerer and feared him. They saw his indignation and shrank back, terrified. He restrained himself by remembering the wretched conditions in which the people had been living for the last several days.

He picked Viviane up and carried her to his horse. The child, still scared, couldn't let go. He had to loosen her hands from around his neck.

He reached into his leather saddle pack for some bread and handed her his water bottle. She devoured the bread, telling him she couldn't remember the last time she'd eaten. He made her eat all of it. Several knights brought the child more provisions.

"Would you like to come with me?" he asked. He told her that he would protect her, care for her, and love her as a father.

"Yes, Master, please," she said. She raised her arms and he enfolded her as she began to cry again, face buried in the giant sorcerer's robe.

A knight brought her a horse that had belonged to one of the thieves. She rode from the town with the King and Myrthynne, holding the sorcerer's hand whenever she could.

She didn't look back.

That night his attendants bathed and clothed her. The women took great pleasure in washing, then brushing the child's lovely hair until it shone with amber glory.

When the attendants brought her to Myrthynne's chambers, her beauty stunned him. Her excitement to be with him in the great king's court touched and pleased him.

She ate a supper of meat, bread, fruits and vegetables. She slept in a real bed in the chamber next to his.

Just before dawn the next day, Myrthynne heard Viviane screaming. He rushed to her chamber and woke her from a terrifying nightmare. She hugged him, weeping, and told him that she had dreamed of Nehushtan.

Myrthynne began her apprenticeship as soon as he could, teaching her the mysteries of the Cymreig. She also learned to read, write, and do mathematics. He taught her mythology and the history of Faerae. The child proved herself bright, willing, eager and earnest.

The dreams and the horror that came with them continued each night, however. Then, one morning she came to his chamber, beaming. "Master," she said.

"Beloved?" he asked, amused.

"I have a new friend. A dream friend."

"Yes?"

"Yes. I call him Gareth. We fought Nehushtan together last night. We drove him off." Myrthynne managed to keep smiling, but he knew who, or what had invaded the child's dreams. The terror would plague her the rest of her life. He embraced the girl, stroking her hair and letting her know the pride he felt in her.

Denied children of his own, he adopted her and she became the pride of his life. She and the great wizard came to love each other as father and daughter.

Myrthynne let go of the precious memories, returning to

the clearing where he hid with Viviane and Gareth. "Beloved," said Myrthynne, shaking off his memories. "Help me to the cave, child." He leaned on her and Gareth while they walked.

Gareth, the blond Welsh knight with sapphire eyes, had fallen in love with Viviane. He knew about the Cymreig. He didn't understand it, but he didn't fear it, either. He regarded it as part of the girl he loved.

The sorcerer needed to hide, he knew. The final battle loomed just ahead, inevitable and fatal. He couldn't be destroyed, however. He had a fate that transcended the need of the King.

First, though, Myrthynne had to make sure Viviane understood her danger. She had to keep the Cymreig safe and pass it on to her children. She also had to protect it from Nehushtan.

Myrthynne would remain suspended between life and death, between sleep and consciousness. He would wait, lying on a cedar bed, sealed within the crystal cave. "Viviane," he said. "The Cymreig must not be lost. Take Gareth and this money and go to Ireland. You must escape the bastard Mordred."

"I can't leave you."

"You must. He will kill you. Hide in daylight, travel at night. Avoid main roads."

"I am afraid."

"Gareth will protect you always. Marry and have children. Some of them will have the Cymreig."

The girl agreed, and took Myrthynne's hand for the last time. He looked into her eyes, which filled with tears. She found the right place in his mind and she Paiked.

She would pass the knowledge on to her children who would be born with the ability. The link to Myrthynne would pass to her children and their children.

He felt Viviane's horror as the Cymreig revealed the Snake, waiting, eager to destroy her and her offspring. She could hide from Mordred and his mercenaries in Ireland. But the Snake would always pursue her and her progeny. She moaned with dread.

"I will try to protect you and your children," the wizard thought to her. "One of them will know that the time has come and will wake me when I am needed again."

He removed a ring from his little finger and slipped it onto her ring finger. The ring, a gold band, had two lovely emeralds flanking a magnificent diamond. "Keep this safe, Beloved Viviane. It has a history from antiquity. Now go. Be at peace."

He showed her the plan for escape. They smiled together with anticipation.

She said the words that would put him into the Sleep. Myrthynne closed his eyes.

Myrthynne felt the mind link diminish, though it did not sever. Some of his mind would always remain with her. They would communicate through the Cymreig until the moment she died.

He would, on occasion, reach out with his mind to help Viviane or one of her children. He would link with them and send help. Once in a while he'd work through someone who didn't have the Cymreig. Whenever the Snake would attack, he would intervene. The Snake liked destruction and chaos.

If Nehushtan and his minions could defeat and eradicate the Cymreig, pandemonium would reign.

Myrthynne, using the Cymreig, watched Viviane and Gareth laboring to pile stones at the cave's entrance. At night they rode toward the coast. She journeyed on Regulus, Myrthynne's grand war charger, a gift from the king. Gareth rode Bayard, a horse given to him by his older brother Gawaine.

That night, two fugitives walked into the Mercenary camp. The old man and the young woman made no attempt to escape or to free themselves.

The captors brought them before Mordred, who kept a respectful distance. He ordered his men to blindfold the two sorcerers, knowing the power in those green eyes.

He condemned them to death but couldn't resist taunting the old man he feared so much. "The King's tutor," he sneered in his lisping, cynical voice. "The witch who enchants people with his eyes."

The old man's expression and posture showed neither fear nor dismay.

"Mordred, the traitor." The old man's voice rang through the clearing. "The son who strikes at his father. You will never wear the crown. You will die at the hands of your own father."

The voice terrified the mercenaries. Several moments of silence passed until Mordred broke the silence. He cleared his throat. "You and your whore daughter—once as dangerous as you, they say—will not stand in my way. <u>My</u> *father*"—he sneered the word—"will die. You haven't the power to stop me. Take the girl," he ordered the Viking soldiers. "Burn her.

Let the wizard watch. Then, burn him."

Some men tied the young woman with the blaze of red hair to a stake. They piled brush and kindling and dry brittle straw around her. She stared ahead, calm and fearless. The killers brought the old man forward to watch his apprentice die.

The executioner, his face covered with a black hood, came forward with a flaming brand. He touched the torch to the kindling in thirteen places, as witch-burning tradition dictated. The fire caught and spread. The mercenaries licked their lips in visceral anticipation.

The flames shot up. The young woman didn't scream or yell or twist against the ropes that bound her, rather to the disappointment of the assembled group of hired killers.

The fire surged up to engulf her. The flames blocked her from their vision for some moments. They shielded their faces from the intensity of the blaze.

When the flames died down, they expected to see her charred remains. The stake held a few charred remnants of the ropes dangling from the cross-members. Of the girl they saw not the faintest trace that she had ever existed.

"Where did she go, Sorcerer?" demanded Mordred.

"She went somewhere safe, where you cannot touch her," replied the old man.

"Very well," said Mordred, after a pause to catch his breath. "We will witness his death. He will not get away."

A soldier with a long handled war ax offered to execute the old man. The mercenaries erected a makeshift platform. A stump of oak served as the chopping block.

The old man ascended the scaffold. The guards positioned

him kneeling with his head on the block. The killer swung the ax.

The ax bit into nothing but wood. The old man vanished as fog before a sudden wind. The mercenaries never saw him again.

The real Viviane rode with Gareth to the coast and took passage to Ireland. She married Gareth.

Two of her children were born with the Cymreig but one of them perished in a fearful accident. At least, the people of Viviane's village called it an accident.

But she knew the terrible truth. The Snake would follow her children wherever they went.

"My gosh," said Therese. "Was Viviane my great grandmother, too?"

"I don't know," said McKenna. "Gayle?"

"That's the tradition, yes," said Gayle. "I know, however, that the Cymreig existed in other families than ours."

"Yes," said McKenna. "It's a mark of Faerae, as I say."

"Does this ability spring into being at once?" asked Therese. "I mean, as soon as you're born?"

"I don't know," Gayle said. "That's the way it's always happened to my knowledge."

"Me too," said Clint. "I tried to repress it, mostly because my parents held me in such contempt because of it."

"My mom's stepsisters hated her, too," said McKenna. "I've never met them. They have no interest in having anything to do with her."

"I mean, could I acquire it?" asked Therese.

"Probably not," said Gayle. "You have faerae blood, yes, but you don't have the green eyes."

Therese bit her lip. "I'd like to help you two," she said.

"I know," said Gayle. "But let's just see what happens."

"This is dangerous, though," said Steve, entering the cabin.

"Why?" asked Therese.

"We're dealing with forces we don't understand," said Gayle.

"But you and Clint—" began Therese.

"—have never encountered anything like this," said Clint. "Never."

"Okay," said Therese.

Arcturus plowed through increasing surge, now at 25 to 30 foot waves. It began to get dark. "Therese?" asked Steve. "Shall we head for home?"

"I wish we could anchor and set out from here in the morning," she said.

"I know," he said. "But we can keep going if you want."

Therese consulted with the group, but everyone was willing to go along with the plan. Steve said he'd stay on the bridge and sleep later. "Thanks a lot," said Therese.

"Therese, I've been learning about running the ship, steering, navigation, and so on…"

"Yes?" said Therese.

"So, I'm pretty confident I can handle the ship," said Clint. Steve nodded and agreed.

"I'll come along about midnight," said Clint. "You and Clovis take the first shift." Steve said okay.

* * * * *

McKenna jerked awake. She looked at her wrist watch wondering, *What woke me up?* The clock read 1:45. She reached next to her and felt Clint still in bed.

"Clint!" she whispered, and he came awake.

"Boy oh boy," he yawned. "Midnight already?"

"No," she said. "1:45."

"What!" he said, coming awake. "Why didn't the alarm go off?" He yanked on his running shoes and ran toward the bridge, McKenna right behind him.

The ship was adrift, powered down, as far as they could see. The bridge lay open, lights off, and they ran inside. Clint verified that the ship was adrift and the engines were turned off.

"Where the heck are Steve and Clovis?" asked Clint as he powered up the engines and brought the ship on course heading into the wind. "Jeez, we're lucky we didn't heel over. What was he thinking of?"

"Steve wouldn't leave the bridge unattended," said McKenna. "Certainly not in high seas and inclement weather."

McKenna raced to her friend's cabin. She banged on the door again and again. At last a sleepy Therese opened the door.

"Mickey," she mumbled. "Is the ocean on fire?"

"Where's Steve?" McKenna interrupted.

"He isn't on the bridge?" asked Therese, still stupid with sound sleep.

"No!" McKenna yelled. "Therese, wake up! We're in danger!"

Therese came alive. She shook her head, then turned to the washstand and splashed some cold water in her face. "Wait," said Therese. She leaned back into the cabin and turned on the light. "He isn't in bed," she said. "I'll check the washroom." She came back in a second, looking fearful.

"He isn't there, either," she said.

Therese tied a bathrobe and led a sprint to the bridge. "He's not back?" she asked Clint.

"No," said Clint, wrestling with the wheel. "We're doing all right. It's tough, and I'm not a great seaman, either."

Arcturus staged a gradual recovery. Clint brought it to bear on its former course and the great yacht began to cut a smooth track through the waves. "How high are they?" asked McKenna.

"20-30 feet," nodded Clint. "I think we'll be okay now, though. Why don't you two go to find Steve?"

"Did you try to sense him?" asked McKenna.

"Yeah, but no luck," said Clint. "I don't sense him anywhere."

"You mean he don't think he's on board the ship?" asked Therese. Clint nodded. "Where could he go?"

"I don't have a clue," said Clint. "What about Clovis?"

"I'm here," said Clovis. He walked onto the bridge, holding his head with both hands. "Someone brained me and pushed me outside. I woke just before I rolled overboard. Someone paiked me and brought me back to consciousness."

Clint stared at him for a moment. "Paiked you? Who did that? And how do you know about the Paik?"

Clovis stared at him. "I'm—er – a Cymrieg, Clint. Like you."

Therese and McKenna stared. "Why haven't you told us before?" asked Therese.

"Hang on a minute," said Clint. "Go find the others. Clovis, help me out."

The two women nodded and ran from the bridge. "Let's stay together, Therese," said McKenna.

"Right," agreed Therese.

They checked first the galley, then crew quarters. Therese became more and more frightened.

At last they ran into the dining room. The room was dark except for a tiny light on the coffee machine. Therese threw on the lights.

"Mom!" she yelled, spotting Gayle slumped on the table. Gayle didn't move. Therese ran to her and shook her. Gayle slumped and opened her eyes.

"Therese," she said. "I'm awake. Where's Steve?"

But now she saw McKenna kneeling on the other side of the table. "He's here!" she cried. "Under the table!"

Steve lay unconscious and didn't respond to McKenna and Therese. McKenna wet a cotton napkin with cool water while Therese and Gayle laid him on his back. McKenna wiped at his face with the cloth until Steve began to respond. His eyelids fluttered, then he squeezed his lids together and forced them open. "Steve!" said Therese.

"Therese," he said. "What on earth?"

"We fought them off," said Gayle.

Steve thought for a few seconds, and then appeared to remember. "Right," he said. "They came for me on the bridge."

"I'll be right back," said McKenna. She ran from the galley dining room.

McKenna ran to the bridge and found her husband wrestling with the wheel. "Found them," McKenna said.

"Right," said Clint. "I had a sense of Steve a few minutes ago."

"They were unconscious in the ward room," she said. A huge wave broke over the bow.

"Unconscious!" he frowned. "What happened?"

"I don't know," his wife said. "They were just coming around down there."

Steve and Therese entered the bridge. "You okay?" Steve asked Clint.

"Sure," he said. "We got high waves, but she's handling it okay."

"Right," mumbled Steve.

"What happened?" Clint asked him.

"I haven't a clue," he said. "I was getting ready to come to get you. Then I was waking up in the ward room."

"Clovis?"

"I almost rolled overboard," Clovis said. "I know someone paiked me."

"Me too," said Grace. "No one's ever done that to me."

"I'm the only Cymreig I've ever met," said Clovis. "But I'm still sure that's what happened to me."

"Did you see something?" Clint asked.

"When I woke up, I had a strange memory of the bridge," he said. "But the memory has faded like a dream. I can't remember."

Now Gayle came in, holding her head against a pounding headache. "Steve," she cried. "Are you all right?"

He nodded and told her his story.

Clint said, "I don't know why I wasn't affected. Maybe because I was asleep? This paik doesn't work when we're asleep, then?"

"Let me ask you something," said Therese. "If this – whatever it is – can do this to you two, what defense do we have against it?"

"I don't know," said Clint. "But I do know that it is afraid."

"Afraid!" said McKenna.

"Yes, I agree," said Gayle. "Without doubt. It feels us coming, and fears that we will disturb the complacency to which it has become accustomed."

"What do you mean?" asked Therese.

Gayle thought for a second. "Well, think about Scrooge in Dickens' *Christmas Carol*. Without reviewing the whole thing, why would someone cut himself off from the world so completely, hoarding, grasping, miserable but unable to rally himself to change his misery?"

"Scrooge wanted revenge on the world," said McKenna. "He was going to show them that they had hurt him, God had hurt him, and he hadn't had the life he thought he was entitled to—"

"Steven King writes about this in *The Shawshank Redemption*, also," noted Steve.

"This from you?" teased his wife. "I didn't know you could read."

"Oh, on occasion I'll get tired of the phone book and comic books, yeah," said Steve. He and Clint rolled their eyes in some amusement. "Anyhow King talks about one of the characters who's released after many years. Instead of embracing his freedom, he can't stop living as a prisoner. Finally he hangs himself, you remember. Then, the character named Red--"

"The book's narrator," nodded McKenna.

"Yeah, right," said Steve. "Once he's released, he begins to think about committing a crime so he can go back into prison where things make sense, as he says."

"Maybe that's what happening here, yes," said Gayle. "We have someone trying to keep us away to preserve his life, such as it is, the way it is."

"But they're in Hell," said McKenna. "Or the next thing to it, right?"

"Yeah," said Clint. "It's not a pleasant place to be."

Gayle nodded. "I felt a terrific relief when we got away from there."

"Look, here's an idea," said McKenna. "Why don't you try to get in touch with this person and bring him here?"

"Huh?" said Therese. "How could they do that?"

"I don't know," said McKenna. "But not much has made sense here. Someone's soul has been stolen, the one who did it died, you got smacked and knocked unconscious — "

"You're right, of course," said Gayle. "What do you say, Clint?"

"I'm willing to try," said Clint.

The ship had been cutting through the waves, but now they noticed that the storm had abated to a considerable extent. It was still pitch dark, but now they noticed that the clouds had begun to part. They could see stars above the clouds, and now the moon, which was full tonight.

"Was this storm an illusion too?" asked McKenna.

Gayle nodded. "Are you ready, Clint?"

He nodded. They locked arms and looked south. In a few moments, they staggered a little. McKenna supported her husband and Steve took Gayle's arm. Then, at once, they gasped and took a step backwards.

Now a small man stood on the bridge, dressed in the outfit of a sailor from centuries before. He drew a deep breath as he gazed around. "Who are you?" he asked in English.

"I am Therese McNulty," she said. "I own this vessel."

He nodded. "How did you call me here?" he asked.

"I did that," said Gayle, "along with this man here."

He gazed at them with remarkable intensity. "You have the Cymreig, then," he said.

"Yes, we do," said Clint. "Though we don't have the profound ability that you do."

He arched an eyebrow. "Yes," he said. "I've been working on it for some time."

"How long?" asked Gayle.

"I don't know," he said. "I only hear shadows, whispers of the world beyond the ship."

"What year do you think it is?" asked Therese.

He shrugged. "It's the second decade of the twenty-first century," said Clint.

Their guest stared for a few moments. Then he managed a nod.

"Everyone I know is many years dead," he said. "Centuries, in fact. If you are speaking the truth."

"Paik me and see," suggested Clint.

The sailor did as he suggested. He nodded again. "What do you want?"

"We would like to rescue her father from your ship," said McKenna. "He swapped his soul with someone on *Fleigende Hollander*."

The sailor looked into her eyes. "Ah yes," he said. "Oosterhuis. I don't know him well."

"After three or four centuries you don't know everyone on the ship?" asked Gayle in some surprise.

The sailor sighed. "Every day is exactly the same," he said. "Every day we fight the same storm. We have to man our stations, haul the lines, swab the decks. We are granted no time to talk, to get to know one another. We sleep, we wake up, we do the same thing day after day."

"But you are aware that time is passing the world," said Therese.

The sailor shrugged. "I am," he said, "because of the Cymreig. No one else senses time passing. I tried to tell people, but to no avail. They don't have the ability to look beyond the ship and the day."

"Why have you sent us these visions?" asked Steve.

The man turned to him. "Do you command this vessel, then?"

"Steve," said Gayle in an undertone. "Be very careful what you say."

"What is your name?" asked Steve.

"Van Brandt," said the man.

"You didn't answer my first question," said Steve. "Why have you tried to scare us off?"

"Why would you approach?" Van Brandt asked. "The ship is lost, our crew is lost. What could you do?"

"Perhaps save my father," sniffed Therese.

Van Brandt gave a little snort. "I doubt that you can help him," he said. "He has chosen an eternity with a ship of evil, one that can never reach shore, much less come home. He's thinking he's gained eternal life, when it's merely eternal tedium."

"And you've lived with this for centuries yourself," said Clint.

A look of profound sadness overcame the sailor. "Yes," he said. "I can think of nothing that could redeem us. I have learned to use the Cymreig more and more, so that I can roam away from the ship, as I am doing now. I can construct other realities for myself."

"But this punishment shouldn't apply to the whole crew," said Therese. "Only the captain cursed God, isn't that correct?"

"No," whispered Van Brandt. "Many people vanished from the ship at once and then over the years. I think they were the ones who were redeemed in life, or learned somehow to pray. The rest of us…" his voice trailed away.

"Where is the ship now?" asked Steve. "On the bottom?"

Van Brandt shook his head. "No," he said. "It drifted south, and eventually became locked in the ice at the southern ice pack—"

"We call it Antarctica," said McKenna.

"Yes," said Van Brandt. "It became frozen in the ice."

"Can you lead us to it?" asked Steve.

"I can," said Van Brandt. "But I'm not sure you want to go there."

"I've been there," said Gayle.

"And I," said Clint.

"You mean with the Cymreig," said Van Brandt. They assented. "What would you do if you find it?"

"Try to find my father," said Therese.

"Mr. Van Brandt, could you help us find him?" asked McKenna.

"I think so," he said. "Do you have a map?" he asked, turning to Steve.

Steve gave him a map of Antarctica. The sailor pointed to a cape near the edge of the ice pack nearest to South Africa.

He turned to the group. "Very well," he said. "I don't have much time. Please be careful. I will help you if I can.

Meanwhile, be aware that this will be a great challenge."

"Is the ship in any way salvageable?" asked Clint.

"I don't know," Van Brandt said. "It hasn't rotted much. After all, it has been frozen in the ice. You might be able to chisel your way aboard."

"Thank you for your—" began Therese, but Van Brandt no longer stood on the bridge of *Arcturus*.

Chapter Twenty-One

"What now?" asked McKenna.

"I think we need to go back to Cape Town and get some cold weather gear," said Therese.

"Is that going to be easy?" asked McKenna.

"I don't know," said Therese.

"Why don't we have some supplies sent to us?" asked Clint. "I could order some cold weather gear, some dynamite, picks and shovels…"

"Yeah, that's a good idea," said Steve. "It could be waiting for us at Cape Town when we get there."

Clint and Steve began to make a list of materials they thought they'd need. Clint used his cell phone to order the material and had it air mailed to Therese's office in Cape Town. Meanwhile, Steve headed the *Arcturus* back to Cape Town.

Clint and McKenna went to bed early that night. Before they slept, McKenna leaned up on one elbow. "Okay," she said. "What are we into this time?"

He shrugged. "This is a chance to help some men redeem their souls," he said. "I have the feeling that we're called into this like we were with the other trip, you know. Maybe it's time to help someone else out again."

"What do you mean?"

"What's a better thing to do with a life?"

"Right," she said. "But I don't think I've given enough to you."

He thought for a second. "Is this about a family again?"

She giggled and whacked him. "No," she said. "At least, not directly."

"How do you mean?" he smiled.

"Look," she said, after thinking for a few moments to compose a reply. "You know what I remember most when I think about my parents?"

"What they did for others, I guess," Clint said, after thinking it over another brief time.

"Exactly," said McKenna. "I think of how my mom and dad support so many charities, their volunteer work, and my dad directing plays with kids."

"My parents never did any of that. They hoarded, connived, never gave to the needy, and so on."

"Well, they certainly have never treated you well," she sniffed.

"I've tried to be understanding with that," said Clint. "They had a child with an absolutely unusual ability who could do things kids normally can't do. I mean, the Cymreig. Before I learned how to control it, I'd slip into their minds and do—this is hard to admit—really nasty things to them."

"Like what?"

"Oh, if they punished me, I'd send them terrible nightmares for days," he said. "It took them a while to figure out what I was doing, but when they did, they tried to force me into their mold of what a person should do and be."

"I see," she said. "Didn't work very well, did it?"

"Oh, I don't know," he said. "Your mom has been helping me understand how to be appropriate when I use the gift, as you know."

"Right," nodded his wife. "I've seen that."

"But one thing she's always told me," said Clint. "The ability increases with use, as you know."

"Right," said McKenna. "That's what Mom has always told me."

"So this man from the ship, Van Brandt, has had far longer to practice this gift than anyone ever has," he said. "I'm not sure Gayle and I would have any luck against him if shove comes to heave, if you take my meaning."

McKenna was silent. "Should we bring in reinforcements?" she asked at last.

He considered. "I don't know who that would be," he admitted.

"Well, my Mom, Mickey Logan, you know," she said. "There's a lot of room on this ship."

Clint looked at her. "Would they come?" he asked.

"I hate to put them in danger, Clint," she said, after a consideration. "But that sort of adventure would appeal to them, I know."

"Why not let them make that decision?" he asked. "We can tell them what they're getting into in advance."

She thought. "Yeah, why not?"

CHAPTER TWENTY-TWO

Mac McNulty had taken all he could. He'd been lashed with the whip several times, now. The infractions for which he received punishment had, to his way of thinking, been minor—stretching his back while scrubbing the deck in a rainstorm of epic proportions; yanking the whip out of the mate's hand; pulling a knife out to cut away a piece of snarled rope instead of untangling it.

The mate with the cane came by as he was bent over, kneeling on the deck, scrubbing at a stubborn spot—the same stubborn spot that he'd scrubbed away the day before—when the mate, Roggins, hit him across the shoulders with the Cat he carried everywhere. Mac looked up and snarled.

"You hit me with that whip again and I'll kick your ass," he told the man. The man looked bewildered for a few moments, trying to decode the unfamiliar expression. Then recovered and swung the whip again. Mac exploded with fury. He hit the man in the stomach with his shoulder and drove Roggins back against the ship's rail.

Roggins gasped as the football block drove his breath out of his lungs. He fell to his knees, but Mac, still blind with fury, yanked him to his feet. Mac smashed his fist into Roggins face, gut, head and shoulders. Roggins fell to his knees, bruised and bloody. "I warned you, Roggins," Mac yelled in his face. "Don't touch me again."

Roggins gasped, and then made a gesture. Before Mac knew what was happening, strong hands has seized him and dragged him up the steps to the quarterdeck. His hands were tied behind him, his legs bound and his hat pulled off and cast aside.

Now the rope. One of the men slid the noose over his head and jerked it tight. In the next moments, Mac McNulty found himself dangling above the deck, thirty feet in the air. He realized that he only had moments to live—

"Get up, Oosterhuis!" bellowed the mate. "The storm is worse! Get up on deck!"

It was a new day. He was not dead, he felt fine, his neck didn't hurt—He'd died the day before, but survived somehow and the whole day had been reset. Again. Just as always.

The full impact of his decision to come to *the Flying Dutchman* hit him full force.

He made his way to the deck, his mind working at a furious rate. He realized the impact of this event. He'd died, yes, but he couldn't stay dead. He could drown himself, slash his wrists, die in a fight with another crewman, anything—

But he wouldn't stay dead. Not now, not ever. For the freedom to live forever, he'd sacrificed a great deal, for more than he would have guessed. He'd never be with a woman again. He'd never make friends again. Never close a deal. Never order a $50.00 steak in a restaurant. Never enjoy a $275.00 bottle of fine wine that matched well with the steak. Never sleep in a comfortable bed in his lavish bedroom, or enjoy a dessert in a foreign port on the back deck of his yacht.

Not only that, but he'd never see the people whom he loved, especially his brilliant, capable daughter. Never. And worse than that, his memory of the world he'd left had begun to fade. He felt himself moving to the point of not being able to remember the life he'd come from in the world in which he'd been born and lived nearly fifty years.

Now, he began to think. Could he find a way out of this? He began to scrub. Then scrub again.

CHAPTER TWENTY-THREE

Arcturus docked two days later. Clint and McKenna went at once to call her parents and her uncle.

"Mom," said McKenna.

"Hi, Honey," said Anna Fixx, and McKenna could hear the smile in her voice. "Where are you now?"

"We're in Cape Town," said McKenna. "How about coming over?"

Silence. "You want me to come there?" said her Mother, and McKenna could hear the smile in her voice.

"Well, let me tell you what's up." McKenna related what was happening to Anna, especially noting the appearance of a Dutch Cymreig. "So we could really use you and Casey here."

"This person has been trapped for centuries?" gasped Anna.

"Yes," said her daughter. "And his control of the Cymreig exceeds anything Clint and Gayle have ever seen."

"I can imagine," said Anna. "Let me call you back, okay?"

McKenna's second call went to her uncle, Mickey Logan, and produced a similar conversation. "So you think we might be able to help all these people?" he asked.

"Yes," said his niece. "Could you and Aunt Karen come?"

"Well, it would be an adventure," he agreed. "A cruise in the south Atlantic, no less."

He also asked for permission to call back.

"Well?" asked her husband Clint when McKenna discon-nected from the phone call.

"I think, I piqued their interest," she smiled.

"You're a born salesman," Clint said.

CHAPTER TWENTY-FOUR

Anna O'Neill lay on her bed with Casey Fixx, whom she loved more than anything in the world. "Casey," she said, and ran her hands along his chest.

"Mm, hm?" he managed, perhaps one inch from slumber.

"Can we talk for a few minutes before you go to sleep?"

"Sure, I guess," he said. She heard, as she always did, the profound love in his voice. Anna smiled. She'd made a bad mistake and been separated from this man for several years. Then, her husband died, she thought. Her reunion with Casey had been forced on her and although bittersweet, they'd rekindled the profound love they felt for one another. She sat up and pulled off her pajamas. Then she lay back down, turned and melted against her husband.

"Whoa!" said Casey with no little enthusiasm. "I thought we were going to sleep now."

She grinned. She loved knowing that no one would ever love her as much as he did. They embraced, and little conversation transpired for several moments. At last, Casey leaned back. He closed his eyes and sighed with contentment.

Then his eyes jerked open.

"Oh, brother," he said.

She leaned up. She placed her hands on his chest and smiled down at him. "What, 'oh brother'?" she asked in her most beautiful North Carolina accent, sounding innocent and as pure as the first snow.

"That was a bribe, wasn't it?" he asked.

She laughed and whacked his chest. "What would you think of going to the South Pole?"

* * * * *

"The South Pole?" Rand Logan gawked. She sat at the kitchen table with Mickey, her husband.

"Well, yeah," he said. "McKenna needs us."

"And we're going after *The Flying Dutchman*? A myth? A legend?"

"I know it sounds crazy," he said.

"Crazy!" she said. "That assertion will live in the annals of Great Understatements."

He didn't speak at first. "I know it sounds ridiculous," he agreed. "But McKenna thinks they may have a clue about its whereabouts."

Karen stared at him speechless for a few moments. "Mickey, I don't know what…" she managed.

He stood and walked to the sink. "Look," he said. "You know about the Cymreig. I've used it with you a few times."

"Sure, I know," she said.

"Look, then," he said. "I think someone on that vessel has a profound gift of the Cymreig. More than anyone other than Myrthynne."

"What!" Rand's mouth fell open.

"I know," he said. "The power increases the more you use it. Since Myrthynne is in something like suspended animation in The Crystal Cave he doesn't age either. So he has the ability, and has had for centuries, in the most extreme sense."

"Should we get him?" she asked.

"No," said Mickey. "Look, he can only leave the cave in a spectral state until the King returns."

"By the King, you mean…"

"Arthur," he said simply.

She sat in silence for a few moments. Then she nodded and shrugged her shoulders. "Will your sister take our kids?"

"I'm sure," he said. "She's only a couple of months along in her pregnancy, and doing well, and she loves having our kids over. She agreed when I called her, and sounded excited."

"Okay," she said. "Call for tickets and let's get packed."

"We're going to need our winter gear," he said. "Long johns, woolens, hats and gloves."

"I thought we were going to South Africa," she frowned.

"I'm afraid we'll be going to the South Pole as well."

"What!"

* * * * *

Mickey and Rand met Casey and Anna at the airport the next morning. Casey and Rand hugged and tried to console one another.

"Some vacation, huh?" Casey smiled.

"Oh, well," Rand said. "I like ocean voyages."

"Yeah, but to the South Pole?" chuckled Casey.

"I guess it's what we deserve for marrying these two," she muttered.

They smiled and followed their spouses onto the plane. The expense of taking along winter gear for McKenna and Clint was high, but Casey shrugged. "She'll pay us back," he smiled.

* * * * *

McKenna and Clint went aboard *Arcturus* and found Therese and Steve and Clovis supervising the loading of the ship. "Good grief," grinned Clint. "Are we moving in at the South Pole?"

"The demolition stuff was hard to secure," said Steve. "I had to get the company involved. Therese's efforts got us what we need."

"Mom and Dad will be here tomorrow, and so will Mickey and Rand," said McKenna. "They're boarding the plane now."

"Okay," said Steve. "We're both grateful, to say the least."

"Mickey," said Therese. "Are we in danger?"

"You mean from Van Brandt?" asked McKenna.

Therese nodded. "I don't understand this Cymreig stuff," she said. "I never knew that a race called Faerae still existed until I met you."

"I know," said McKenna. "I didn't learn about it until I was almost ready to go to college."

"If my Mom has the ability, could I have it too?" asked Therese.

McKenna looked at her friend. "I don't think so," she said. "The mark is someone who has fiery red hair and emerald green eyes. I've got the red hair, but blue eyes. You've got the green eyes, but not the red hair. Still, from what Mom says, the ability turns up once in a while. Like with Mickey. No one in his family except his grandfather had the ability for several centuries."

"So this could turn up in one of my kids?" asked Steve.

"Possible," said Clint. "But impossible to predict, if you understand." Steve nodded.

"One thing I can tell you," said McKenna. "My mom had a miserable relationship with her step sisters, who hated and distrusted her from the time she was little. Casey came as a revelation to her. He loved her without condition, without concern about her ability with the Charm."

"Mickey had the same thing," said Clint. "So did I. Both of us are outcasts in our family, who don't want anything to do with us. My parents and siblings don't want anything to do with me. I haven't laid eyes on them in years. Not even spoken to them."

"Sad," said Steve. "You'd think they'd rejoice that one of their children was special, wouldn't you."

"McKenna and I have loved each other all our lives," said Clint. "The Cymreig pulled us together."

"You talk about it like it was a person," said Steve.

"No, it is no entity," said Clint. "Most of us don't know each other. McKenna's mom and I communicate on occasion, and I do with Mickey, too. Anna's Grampa could do it better than all of us—" Clint paused, considering.

"What?" said McKenna.

"Well, I hadn't thought about it," he said. "I think maybe the reason he became so adept with it was because he had used it for so long. He was almost ninety when he died."

"Hmm," nodded McKenna.

"I gather that you think the four of you—Gayle included—can overcome Van Brandt when we find the ship."

"I don't know," said Clint. "I'm grasping at straws. For one thing, I never heard of anyone from Holland having the gift. For another, there seems to be a brotherhood of us, and –I don't know– sort of a mutual agreement not to use it except to do good."

"Why do you say that?" asked Therese.

"Well, I remember one time when I was a sophomore in college," shrugged Clint. "I used it to smack a guy from a fraternity I belonged to at one point. They'd thrown me out, which isn't uncommon for those of us who are gifted in some way, not just the Cymreig, either. The guy who came to tell me got it over with and started to leave. I gave him a vision of his greatest fear, which was being the victim of a lynch mob."

"Oh, good grief," said Therese.

"Yeah, I know," said Clint. "Normally when I use the Cymreig, I'm tormented for several nights by horrid, vivid nightmares."

"Yech," said McKenna. "Yeah, he isn't great to be around then."

"I apologize all the time, don't I?" he said. She smiled and hugged him.

"Go on with the story," she urged him.

"But with the fraternity guy, I didn't have the nightmares," he said. "The memory of doing it to him haunted me for a long time. I felt terrible."

"Have you overcome this nightmare stuff?" asked Therese.

"Never," he said. "The nightmares became bearable when I married someone who loves me. I can kind of hold on to McKenna to moderate the terror. She visits my dreams and helps me out, drives away the terror."

Therese now got the picture. "Do the rest of the people have the same experience when they use the Cymreig?"

"I think so," he said. "Anna and Mickey for sure. I haven't asked Gayle, but…"

"Haven't asked Gayle what?" said Therese's mom, entering the wardroom and pouring some coffee. Clovis came in behind her and Clint summarized the conversation.

"Yes," said Gayle. "That nightmare stuff holds true for me as well."

"And me," agreed Clovis.

"Can you do this, then?" asked Steve. "If this is an occasion of terror for you, why are we going?"

"Well, for one thing, we might be able to set free a crew of men from their torment," said Clint. McKenna nodded.

"I don't think we can overestimate the terror of an eternity of imprisonment," she said.

"You're right, McKenna," said Gayle. "Humans aren't meant to be slaves. They rebel against it."

"Then let's help them," said Therese.

Chapter Twenty-Five

Picking up McKenna's parents and her aunt and uncle made it necessary to rent a larger vehicle at the airport. While Clint went to retrieve them, Therese and McKenna spent their time helping Clovis setting up a special welcome dinner with African dishes, fruits and wines. The South African wines caused the group to raise their eyebrows with their subtle yet distinctive bouquets, their rich colors and startling savor. Mickey and Karen pronounced them excellent.

After dinner, McKenna and Therese attempted to summarize the voyages in search of Mac McNulty.

"Swapped souls?" said Casey, stunned at the concept.

"It appears so," nodded Clint. "None of us have a clue how this could have happened, though, how he could have learned…" he fell silent, considering.

"What?" said McKenna, when he hadn't spoken for several moments.

"Oh, sorry," he said. "It just occurred to me. I wonder if this guy is the source of the legends about *The Flying Dutchman*. I mean, perhaps he's at the heart of all the legends about the people who die, and lose their souls, and other horrible things with the mythos that goes with it."

"That would make sense," said Anna, his mother-in-law. "Yes, Clint, I agree that the mechanism for swapping souls far exceeds my ability, but also, I wouldn't consider doing such a thing to someone else."

"I imagine that would have to do with the fact that you really don't have a fear of death, Mom," said Clint to his mother-in-law. "I mean, you've become a person of some formidable faith, and you have a knowledge of where your soul will be going upon your death." Anna nodded, appreciating the point.

"But this guy, it seems obvious, does live in terror of dying," said McKenna. "As I consider it, he's been imprisoned for centuries, unable to let life go." Heads nodded.

"We seem to be doing a lot of speculating," said Anna.

"Do we have a choice in how we proceed?" said Steve. "I'm afraid of this guy, I don't mind admitting. If he's more powerful than all of you put together, is there anything we really can do?"

The table fell silent as they considered. At last, Anna spoke up.

"Let's go to Myrthynne," said Anna. Everyone seemed to agree with McKenna's mother. She took the hands of Casey and McKenna, and Mickey took Rand's hand. Gayle took her daughter's face in her hands and looked through her eyes as Therese grasped Steve's hand.

In the next moment, Therese found herself in a cave. She staggered for a moment as she saw the exquisite quartz formation and heard a musical tone. A well in the center of the room bubbled and emitted a beautiful scent into the air.

Therese fell to her knees, hands to her mouth, overwhelmed at the beauty of the surroundings. She saw Gayle, McKenna and Anna embracing a tall man in a monk's cloak. Mickey shook the man's hand and then also embraced him.

"Therese," smiled the huge man. He crossed to her and took her hands. "And this is your husband," he said, gripping the hands of Steve, who smiled and then winced at the strength of the man's grip. Now Clovis joined the group and shook hands with Myrthynne, and embraced him as well.

Therese crossed to them. "Master," she said, "You know me?"

"Yes, Beloved, since you were very little," said the man. "I am delighted that you have come to me." Therese introduced Steve, who felt a little intimidated in the presence of the huge man.

"I have hoped indeed that you would come," said the man. "You have not unlocked the mystery of the Cymreig."

"Master," she said. "Myrthynne."

"Yes, Dearest," he said, and opened his arms. She crossed to him in several steps and fell into his embrace. "At last you have come to me," he said.

"Master," said Anna. "Do you know what we are dealing with?"

"Yes, Viviane," said Myrthynne. "You are in combat against an enemy who should be long dead, who should have died centuries ago."

"Who is he, really?" asked McKenna.

"He is an Irish Cymreig," said Myrthynne. "Most people who have the power make hideous mistakes, as did you, each of one of you." They all nodded, except for Therese. "What makes you different is that you were able to admit it and accept the consequences of your ill-advised actions."

"You mean that people are always afraid of us, or at least, of the power we have?" asked Anna.

Myrthynne nodded. "Yes," he said. "When you have an ability that others do not have, they almost always become jealous of you. Mickey, for example, faced hideous ridicule at the hands of his family who never understood, or wanted to understand, his ability. Nor did he have success making and keeping close friends until he met Karen, likewise creative and artistic." He smiled at Mickey and his wife, who returned his grin.

"But I had Grandpa," said Mickey, referring to his mother's father, the most precious person in his life. "Also Aunt Sharon who loved and encouraged me. She introduced me to literature, to Shakespeare, to theatre."

"Why are we here, Master?" asked Steve.

"Is it to find another Cymreig?" asked Therese.

"Yes, of course," said Myrthynne. "Other than Mr. Clovis, I can find no other Cymreigs in South Africa, no one who can help you."

"Help with what?" asked Steve, mystified.

"With overcoming and, I fear, destroying the Evil Cymreig Brandt," said Myrthynne. "Yet if he cannot be destroyed, he will continue in this cursed state for eternity and provoke much evil and dismay."

"What can we do, Master?" asked Casey, his face drawn with concern. He wrapped his arm around his wife Anna and held her close as Myrthynne began to speak.

Mac McNulty woke up. Today was the day. Today he was going to end the curse on *The Flying Dutchman*. First he had to set the stage. He dressed in the dark. By now, he knew where the clothes would be every morning.

He had a plan he didn't think could fail. He'd try it out for the first time today. If it worked, so much the better. If it didn't, he'd memorize what he'd done wrong and correct it tomorrow.

It was still dark. No stars, no moon—nothing but deep, profound clouds and rain, as it always was. The waves were terrifying, too: breaking over the top of the deck, washing the deck with green salt water, icy cold and vicious.

He scaled the rope ladder to the crow's nest. He'd watched with intensity as the captain, on his way to the top of the mast, stepped on the rope rungs as he made his way to the top. Mac had noted which ones the captain's feet always struck. He went to work, fraying those ropes so they'd break as soon as Van Zeeland stepped on them. With any luck, McNulty thought, as soon as the captain stepped, the rungs would break and plunge him without ceremony into the sea.

Then, McNulty knew, the crew would be confused, stunned. He'd be ready. He'd kill the first officer if he gave any problems, but he didn't think he'd have to. The ship would follow him, just like every group he'd ever taken over did.

The sun wouldn't rise, of course. The storm was far too black. Still, that worked in his favor. No one would see him aloft.

He found himself amazed at his own agility. This Oosterhuis must have been an amazing athlete. McNulty could do things he'd never dreamed of. Heights didn't terrify McNulty, either, though in his former life he'd been terrified even to drive over bridges. His knuckles would turn snow white until he crossed the bridge.

This'll be something to tell Gayle and Therese about, he grinned. They'll get a kick out of how he'd won this situation. He'd never killed anyone, at least in a direct sense, though several people had perished with broken hearts at having their companies ripped away from them. This was a new step for Mac, even so. It was no less than coldblooded murder but, he told himself, it was in a good cause.

It would save many men from centuries of anguish, of unproductive lives, of heartbreak.

Mac resolved anew this morning. He had to kill the Captain. No one else could, no one had the least idea of what was happening, nor had they any vision of life without enslavement on a ghost ship.

Okay. This was going to work.

He finished sabotaging the ropes, with the knife he found. It was on the deck every morning, in exactly the same place. Down the netting he scrambled. He could do this in his sleep, he knew. He avoided the sliced ropes without difficulty. Down to the deck and to the galley, where he looked for something to eat.

Mac began to adjust his mind. He had to move from serving on board to leading a crew, and commanding the ship. He'd have to move fast. He found his musket, checked to make sure it was loaded and hid it near the bridge.

An hour went by, and he scrubbed the deck. He scrubbed it again. Then he scrubbed it again.

He sensed the moment had come. He climbed to his feet, seized a rope, and cast it over a sorry looking man standing by the railing. Then he tied it off.

"What is this, Oosterhuis?" demanded the man.

"You'll see," said Mac. "Don't remove the rope."

He crossed the quarterdeck and sat, tying himself to a mast. He didn't have long to wait. The huge wave hit, as it did every day, and washed over him. In the next instant it hit the sailor he'd tied to the railing. The ship rose and the wave washed over the deck.

The man stared at him. "You saved my life, Oosterhuis," he gasped.

"Yes," smiled Oosterhuis.

"How…" the man started. "How could you have known?"

"Never mind," said Mac, and returned to his work. He noticed a strange sensation. He'd helped someone out. He'd saved the man's life.

Mac McNulty realized that he'd taken a step into a new world. He smiled and realized that he had moisture on his face. It wasn't just sea water that he wiped away.

* * * * *

Another hour went by in a dull wind with driving, pounding rain, and huge freezing waves, as it was every day.

Right on schedule, Van Zeeland came out on deck. "Captain," said the first mate, just as he did every day—which, of course, was the same day. "This storm has become extraordinary even for the Cape of Good Hope. Let's retreat for a couple of days. We can come back when this eruption abates."

"Are you afraid?" asked Van Zeeland.

"Yes, sir," said the first mate. "I am indeed. A storm down here is no laughing matter."

"You fool!" lashed out the Captain. "A few hours and we'll be through. Don't let the men see your cowardice."

"Cowardice!" said the first mate.

The captain sprang to the rigging and began to ascend. Almost every eye followed him. He reached the top—

The rope ladder broke. The captain held on to the rung

above it. One of his hand-holds broke. He screamed defiance at the heavens and reached for another--

It broke. The ship heeled to starboard and the captain's hold was wrenched loose. The captain spiraled screaming through the air, catapulted into the huge swells—

Everything changed in an instant. The sea became calm at once, and the sun shone warmth on freezing, miserable men. A breeze stirred the remains of the pennants, not a gale force wind.

The first mate and the crew stood stunned in disbelief for several moments. The mate recovered some composure. "Men!" the mate screamed. "Get a line…"

"Belay that order!" bellowed Mac.

The first mate turned. He found herself staring at the barrel of a musket. "Belay the order!" yelled Mac. "I am taking command as of this minute."

The first mate backed up.

"The captain has drowned!" said Mac. "The ship has to be our priority!"

The first mate hesitated. Then he nodded. "Aye!"

"We're shipping water!" someone yelled up at them.

"Dump the cargo," Mac yelled. "All of you! Be lively if you want to live!"

For the next two hours spices, cotton, and other goods went over the side. "Captain!" yelled one of the men. "All the cargo has rotted, overnight!"

"All of it?" bellowed the first mate.

"Yes, sir," said the sailor. "I don't understand. It was fine when I checked it last night!"

Mac hid a little smile. The sailor didn't understand that last night, as the man called it, had happened some 400 years before. Explaining things would take some doing, he realized.

Now, however, he had to find a way to keep the rotted old hulk afloat until they could be rescued.

It was fortunate, he knew, that these were seasoned, experienced seaman, capable and knowledgeable about their jobs. He'd have to stay out of their way and let them run the ship.

Men down below worked frantically to staunch the worst leaks and pump out the water.

"We're making progress, Sir!" yelled the mate.

"Sir!" yelled one of the men. "Look at the sails! What happened?"

Mac stopped and looked around.

The ship's sails hung in rags. Instead of a trimmed, handsome craft, everything was a wreck.

"Have we got sail to make the mainland?" asked Mac.

"The sails have been ruined," said a man. "They have rotted away. We're adrift."

"Down below?" asked Mac.

"Yes, we have some cloth," said another. "We might be able to cobble a couple of sails together to move the ship."

"Can we fix them?" asked Mac.

"We will work on it," said the bosun's mate. He turned to Mac and said in a hushed voice, "Are we still cursed?"

Mac shook his head with some violence. "I swear it's not too late," said Mac. He barked orders and the men started to go aloft, but the ropes frayed away as the men touched them. "See if you can patch together some of the cloth that's not hopeless." The sailors knuckled their foreheads and began patching.

Mac yelled at the sailors working in the hold. He shouted encouragement and ran from group to group.

"Aye," nodded Mac. "Bail for your lives! Don't give up!"

The seamen worked like demons. They set up kettles and began boiling tar. Then, they began using the pitch to seal the leaks, stuffing shards of wood into the larger cracks and tarring them over. Other men found pieces of sail cloth that were not rotted away and began patching together sails.

"Head north for the coast," said Mac, placing his hand on the shoulder of the first mate who had managed to repair the tiller.

"Aye sir," said the first mate, and placed his knuckles to his forehead. He turned toward Mac and gave a little nod and smile.

* * * * *

On *Arcturus*, the Cymreigs' heads jerked up and turned south. "Steve," yelled Gayle and she ran to the bridge. Clint trailed right behind her, and Mickey ran up on deck.

"What?" Steve asked in bewilderment.

"That way!" yelled the three Cymreigs, pointing to the west. "Something just happened! Full speed!"

"Are you sure?" asked Steve as he and Clovis sprang into action. The Cymreigs screamed their certainty.

Arcturus all but leapt through the water as Clovis pushed on the throttle and brought the ship to the new course.

* * * * *

Mac returned the mate's salute and knew what had happened. The mate had decided to surrender command to him. *I won*, thought Mac. *I won—*

But then he realized. Wait a moment. This old wreck would have to fight for every yard of ocean it covered. He had to keep the men working and straining, struggling to save their lives in an old, unseaworthy craft--

"Sir!" yelled one of the men. "A vessel!"

The man handed Mac a small glass. He peered through it and saw a fine yacht, a motor launch. Something stirred in his memory. He'd seen this vessel before, but—

"It's making for us, Sir," the man said. "What is it? I've never seen anything like it!"

"Charge the cannons," he ordered.

"We have no gunpowder, Sir," said the gunner's mate. "All of it has been soaked overnight."

Mac ran with the mate to the armory and looked. "It's true," he agreed. "Very well. Break out Cutlasses to repel boarders."

"Sir!" yelled the first mate. "I've never seen a ship move that fast!"

"It's driven by motors," said Mac. "Don't worry."

"Motors!" said several sailors. Mac understood their consternation at seeing a vessel from 400 years in their future. He might as well have told them that angels propelled the oncoming ship.

In a few moments the vessel had come alongside.

"Oosterhuis!" bellowed a man standing on the vessel's top deck. Mac realized that the man was Steve Blair, Captain of *Arcturus*.

"Aye!" he yelled back. "I am in command!"

Blair's mouth dropped open. He exchanged words with a woman standing next to him.

"We're going to throw you a line!" yelled the Captain of the vessel. "Make it secure and we will tow you ashore!"

Mac yelled some orders and the crew sprang into action. Within moments the huge yacht had turned and begun towing the decrepit old vessel toward Cape Town.

Mac looked around. About thirty sailors from the Dutchman now stood staring on deck, stunned at what they were seeing. Now a stunning red-headed woman joined the young woman on the bridge.

"Mac!" the woman shouted.

"Here!" he yelled back. "Gayle, what are you doing here?"

He could see that the woman was overcome for a moment at seeing him. She began to cry, he realized. *She's worried about me,* he thought. *She's <u>been</u> worried about me.*

The sailors were still too surprised to react. Then the first mate came onto the deck. "Captain!" he yelled at Mac. He handed him a glass and pointed to the north. "Strange colors, Sir."

Indeed, another ship had showed up. Mac's mind registered that this ship was a Coast Guard Destroyer, though from which country he wasn't sure at first. Not the US, he noted a few moments later. Now he made out the flag. The ship sailed under the flag of The Republic of South Africa.

"It is all right!" he yelled to the crew. "We're safe!"

The Coast Guard vessel came alongside. Within moments *The Flying Dutchman* had been secured to the larger vessel.

"Captain?" yelled someone from the ship.

"Aye," yelled Mac.

"Do you wish to abandon ship?"

"Aye," he bellowed. "Thank you."

The Coast Guard vessel lowered several rope ladders, and the crew of *The Flying Dutchman* began to leave the worthless wreck. Within twenty minutes all of them were evacuated. The crew wrapped blankets around the survivors of *The Flying Dutchman* and showed them to the warmth of the galley. The crew provided clean, dry clothing for the men, who walked around, looking at the unfamiliar ship, stunned at what they were seeing.

The Coast Guard vessel with the antique vessel lashed to it powered up and headed for Cape Town Harbor.

A man in a white suit, bundled against the cold, greeted the men. "Are you the Captain?" asked this man.

"Yes—I mean, Aye, Sir," said Mac. The man saluted. Mac, self-conscious about the action, knuckled his forehead as he'd seen the Dutch sailors do to him.

"I am the commander of the vessel," said the man. "My name is Westin."

"Sir," said Mac.

"Have I the honor of addressing Captain Van Zeelen?" asked the man.

"No," said Mac. "My name is Oosterhuis. I assumed command today when the Captain died."

Western frowned. "How did he die?" he asked.

"He was going aloft—"

"Yes, we know the legend," said Western. "He has been doing this since the middle of the sixteenth century. What happened this time?"

"Several rungs on the rope ladders broke," said Mac. "He lost his grip and was cast into the sea."

The frown deepened. "Have you inspected these ropes?" asked Western.

"No," said Mac. "The storm and the ship occupied all my

time."

"Do you have any thoughts on why this would have happened now, after all these centuries?"

"No," said Mac. "I haven't thought about it at all. It never occurred to me to think of it. I'm certain that they are frayed and old by now."

"Strange," said the Captain. He gestured to an aide, who led Mac down to the galley and a hot meal of soup and coffee.

Mac looked around at the men sitting at the tables and on the ground. He counted only 25 men.

He felt sure that many more men should have survived. Did they stay on *The Dutchman*? No, that was impossible. He'd been the last one off, he was all but certain. He had to go back onto the ship and check. But the men left behind would be okay, he thought. Cold, for sure.

The crew made their way to the ship's workout area. Blankets and pillows were scattered and several men laid down on mats and fell asleep at once.

Though Mac was desperately weary, he was afraid to sleep. He kept worrying that someone would inspect the ropes he'd cut. He tried to rationalize. No one had seen him go aloft, he felt sure. The night was as black as paving tar when he'd gone aloft.

Then he was afraid that if he slept, everything would vanish. He'd wake to find himself on the *Dutchman* again, lost and abandoned for all time. If this idea hadn't worked, what would he do now?

For now he regretted his decision to swap places with the real Oosterhuis. He had thought that living for all eternity would have been wonderful, never having to step into that valley that led into oblivion.

Now, however, he'd realized that life without challenge, without change, without chance was anathema to him. He hated it. He hated the prospect of living forever as he had been for the last several days. Or was it months? Maybe years?

To his horror, he found that he'd been contemplating suicide. A man couldn't live more than a few minutes in the near freezing ocean. But that begged the question: if he'd tried suicide, and been successful, who was to say he wouldn't wake up in the hammock below decks on the *Dutchman*? Why not? Everything he'd done had been reset automatically when he woke up. It wasn't just the same day. It was *exactly* the same day. The men aboard the ship knew him, said the same things, he scrubbed the same section of deck, he went aloft at the same time, ate the same wretched food, drank his allotment of rum – all in the same order, in the same way.

The other men seemed to be oblivious to their plight. They didn't seem to know they were trapped.

"Oh God, please save me," he said, his first prayer since he was a child. He realized that he was broken and his life meant nothing.

Now, though, he might have a chance. This day was different. Van Zeelen was dead – at least, he'd fallen into the ocean before he could curse God – did that mean anything?

At last, though, exhaustion overtook him and he dozed off.

He dreamed, however. Fiery dreams. Nightmare dreams. Dreams of men falling off a ship into a steel gray, roiling sea. Dreams of seeing Therese, his daughter who was so gifted and talented. Brief flickers of women with whom he'd slept over the last thirty years. One face kept arising again and again, as it had for three decades or more. A beautiful girl named Gayle, who had become an exquisite woman.

Anyone who saw the face of the body that lay on the gymnasium mat would have been surprised to see tears on the cheeks of a grizzled, hardened seaman.

CHAPTER TWENTY-SIX

Therese came aboard the Coast Guard vessel, accompanied by Clovis. They were escorted to the ship's gymnasium, where the sailors had been quartered. The crew looked up as they entered.

"Oosterhuis!" called the Captain, who was escorting them. "Clovis!"

At first, the men looked up without interest. Then, seeing a tall young woman of exceptional beauty standing next to the door, they rose to their feet. Two seaman came forward.

"Therese," one of the seaman mumbled. She took his arm and led him to a room, where she sat him at a table. Clovis embraced the other man and they sat on the mat in the gymnasium, where they began to talk.

She nodded to the Captain and he spoke to someone in the hall. The Captain stepped back and Gayle McNulty entered. She shut the door.

The three people sat at a table, staring at one another. At last Therese said, "Dad?"

Mac stood in silence for a moment, trying to speak. He managed to say, "Yes," in a voice choked with tears. The young woman came around the table and hugged him.

Gayle spoke at last. "So you seem to have won, Mac."

He looked at her. "What do you mean?"

"You've cheated death for a little while, at least," said Therese. "And you've become even wealthier."

Mac hadn't thought about that. "Wealthier?" Then he remembered. The gold, of course. Some of it was his. Twenty-four men had come aboard with him, and the fabulous fortune would be divided among them. The value of gold per ounce would make them all rich.

"Well, I guess you're right," he said.

"What do you want to do?" asked Gayle. "No one will believe you are Mac McNulty."

Now he began to see his dilemma. He was alive, yes. But he was trapped in the body of a seaman who had been dead for centuries. He had no identity. No life.

"Are you all right?" said Therese.

"What do you mean?" he mumbled.

"Your health, Dad," she said.

"I think so," he said. "The Coast Guard doctor looked me over and said I seemed okay. I guess I have to go to a hospital when we get to Cape Town." Now it occurred to him. "What about Oosterhuis?"

"Dead," said Gayle. "He died a few days ago. Or, to be more accurate, his soul and your body died. "

"So I am trapped here," said Mac.

"In one sense," said Therese. "On the other hand, you're free for some time."

Mac thought for a second. "What does that mean?"

"It appears that you have a fine body," said Therese, and Gayle nodded.

"Yes," she said. "Oosterhuis must have been strong, judging by his muscles."

"He was very agile, also," nodded Mac. "I'm amazed at the way I can climb ropes, balance way above the deck, walk on the pitching ship."

"It appears that he was in his early forties when he came aboard the ship," nodded Gayle.

"Yes, I think so," agreed Mac. "But he's strong, and in fine condition."

"Do you want to come back to *Arcturus*?" asked Therese.

"No," said Mac. "I'm going to stay with the men. I think I need to start teaching them how to live in this century."

* * * * *

Steve and Therese stood on the bridge of *Arcturus* as he tracked the Coast Guard Destroyer. "Is your Dad scarred by this experience?" asked Steve.

Therese thought. "Not only scarred," she said at last. "I think he's been changed, also."

"How's that?"

She considered her words. "Dad has spent his whole adult life doing what he wants," she said. "He's indulged himself right along—food, women, expensive liquor, all that. I don't know what's happened to him, but he's going to try to become a teacher and help the *Dutchman* crew assimilate to the society. He also wants to take them back to Holland to see what has happened since they left there."

"How is he explaining what happened since they've been gone?" asked Steve.

"I don't know," she admitted. "I think he's just kind of telling the truth."

"Therese," he said. "Let me ask you something. Did he kill Van Zeelen?"

Therese bit her lip. "Yes, I'm sure he did," she acknowledged, after a few moments.

"Has he ever murdered someone before?" her new husband asked.

"Not to my knowledge," she said. "On the other hand…" her voice faded away.

"Yes?" he prodded when she didn't go on.

"Steve, he killed several men, not directly, but indirectly," she said. "When he'd take over a company, he'd displace people who'd been there for years, who'd started the organization maybe, whose lives were focused on their company."

"Right," he said. "He certainly treated me and my crew like we were insignificant, mere blips on the radar, things just like his servants."

"And some people can't survive when all that their lives mean, all they've pointed toward, has vanished with a few strokes of a pen," Therese shrugged.

"You mean Van Zeelen stood in his way, then?"

"Yeah, I think so," said Therese. "On the other hand, Van Zeelen had the primary responsibility to look out for his men. His actions condemned many men to centuries of misery, despair, and fear. They haven't had a moment free from that fear for centuries."

"Was Van Zeelen a mass murderer, then?"

"You do raise a good point," nodded Therese. "Is the hangman who springs the trap, or the electrician who throws the switch, or the drug company that supplies the lethal injection as much a murderer as the one who stands condemned?"

"I don't know," said Steve. "It's not surprising that Mac grew tired of the Dutchman almost at once. He said that he was beaten many times by the bosun's mate. He couldn't defend himself, because of the nature of ship's discipline. They hanged him once."

"And he isn't dead?"

"No," said Steve. "No, he woke up in his hammock the next morning, which was of course the *same* morning, and he was fine."

Therese bit her lip. "It sounds like no one on the ship could bring this torture to an end, doesn't it," she said. "So Dad had to act."

"I don't know," Steve said. "I don't have a clue what the morality is." Therese shrugged.

The Flying Dutchman, in tow with the Coast Guard destroyer, headed for dry dock at Cape Town harbor. The gold would be offloaded into a vault. Clint and McKenna went with Mac to the hold and viewed the bullion. It was a fabulous treasure.

The amount had staggered the young couple, though both of them had seen treasure before. "But nothing like that," said McKenna. "This hold has enough here to make everyone rich."

Therese and Steve didn't know how the money from the gold would be spent or invested. "I don't know for sure," said Steve. "I think that by the laws of salvage, it belonged to the crew that brought it in."

"But these are pretty humble men," said Therese. "They have no clue what to do with new wealth, let alone staggering amounts of gold."

Steve nodded. "You know, something strange seems to be happening, also."

"What's that?" asked Therese.

"How many men went aboard the Destroyer?"

Therese shrugged. "I'm not sure," she said. "I think twenty some, including Dad."

"Where are the rest of the crewmen, then?"

Therese opened her mouth to respond, couldn't, and then tried again. "How many would you expect to be there?"

"Well, the *Dutchman* was a state of the art ship once," said her husband. "I don't know, but I would have thought more than that."

"Why?"

"Ships of that kind had what were called 'watches,'" Steve said. "You'd work for four hours at a time, except when the Captain called an emergency and needed all hands. Once the sails were set, a small group could run the ship, so things had to be found for the others to do. That's why they would scrub decks, paint, repair, and so on. But to respond to an emergency, it seems like you'd need a lot more than just a handful of men."

Therese nodded. "The theory being 'Idle hands are the devil's playthings.'" Steve agreed.

Gayle came over and greeted them. They walked into the room where they found Mac working with the men.

She thought. "You remember when Brandt, the Cymreig, came aboard, he told us that several vanished, as if they were taken away."

"Yeah, I guess," he said.

"How many are there now?"

Steve counted. "I get a couple of dozen."

"Where are the others?"

Steve paused. "I don't know," he admitted. "Not a clue."

Mac came over, smiling. "They seem to be doing well," he said. "They are stunned by the idea that the world is not what they thought it was. But they can see this ship, see the technology, and they have to accept things that are difficult."

Gayle said, "Mac."

He turned and smiled. "What?"

"How many men were aboard the *Dutchman*?" she asked.

Mac did a bit of a double-take. "What do you mean?"

"A ship like that should have had a lot more seaman aboard than those standing here," she said. "What happened to them?"

"They're all here," he said. "Every man I knew on the ship is here."

"How could two dozen men sail a ship as large as the *Dutchman*?" asked Steve.

Mac gave a little stare to the Captain of his yacht. "I don't know," he said. "Are you saying some are missing?"

"It doesn't seem logical that they aren't here," Therese shrugged. "Did any remain aboard the ship?"

"Well, I didn't check below decks," admitted Mac.

"I think I'm going to take Mickey and Anna over there and have a look around," said Steve. "We'll dock in a few moments, and we can go aboard."

"Let's bring Clovis along, too," said Therese.

Mac looked uncomfortable. "You want me to come along?"

"Well, you know the ship a great deal better than we do," Steve agreed.

"Okay, if you want," Mac said.

"Dad," said Therese. "Did you know a man named Brandt?"

"Who?" asked Mac.

"Brandt," repeated Therese. She gave description of him.

Mac thought. "No," he said. "Can't say I ever saw him. How would you know about the names of anyone on that ship?"

"He has the Cymreig," said Gayle. "He came to *Arcturus* before we found you."

"Hmm," frowned Mac. "Excuse me for a second."

He walked over to the seamen, who were talking in quiet groups. Gayle, Therese and Steve saw the men's faces take on the same puzzled expression as Mac had. All of them shook their heads. Mac came over to his daughter's group again.

"No one here has any memory of such a man," said Mac.

When the group recovered a bit, they went to the men and asked them to come to the top deck. "The Coast Guard Destroyer is going to dock in a short time," Gayle told them. "You'll want to see the ship come in and dock."

The men smiled. They came up on deck and saw the skyline of the modern, sophisticated city appear on the horizon.

Mouths dropped open, and tears began to flow. McKenna, Therese and Gayle, along with Anna and Rand, took their arms and tried to comfort them. One man turned to McKenna. "Everything I knew is gone, isn't it?" he asked.

"Yes," she said. "But with your share of the gold, you are wealthy beyond the dreams of avarice. You'll make new friends. You'll build a new life." He nodded but didn't speak.

Ships, yachts and other craft lined the harbor to welcome the ancient vessel to its new home. Ship's horns blew, fireboats shot spray into the air, confetti and pennants flew in the air.

Once the Destroyer docked, a salvage crew went to work lifting the old ship into dry dock. It would never sail again, and would find a permanent home in the harbor of Cape Town.

The crewmen of *the Flying Dutchman* went ashore and were put into quarantine almost at once. It would take some effort to stabilize their immune systems.

Chapter Twenty-Seven

McKenna sat with her mother on the deck of *Arcturus*.

"Mom, I'm very puzzled," she said.

"Yes?" said Anna Fixx.

"We had a Cymreig show up on the ship," she said. "That's why I asked you to come. He drew a map that led us to *The Dutchman*. Clint and Gayle Paiked him, and he Paiked them back. They felt there was no doubt that he was genuine."

"Okay—" Anna began.

"But then we found the ship—or it found us, whatever—and the Cymreig wasn't on board. Nor did Gayle or Mickey have a sense of him. The sailors we talked to don't remember him, either."

Anna thought for a few moments. "He could be a ghost, maybe," said Anna. "If so, he doesn't leave a trace if he's gone into the abyss."

"So why can we remember him?"

"Well, you did see him, right?" she asked.

"Yeah, for sure."

Anna cleared her throat. "That's a difficult situation," she said. "Let me get Clint and Mickey and we'll go back to the vessel."

Two hours later McKenna and Clint went aboard the old ship. McKenna had never been on the ship and found herself holding her husband's hand. "You scared?" he asked, sounding a little amused.

"Damn right," she said. "This has been a ghost ship for centuries."

"Speaking of which," he said.

"Hmm?"

"How many seaman are left?" he asked.

"Still about twenty, I think," she said. "I didn't check today."

He shook his head. "It could be that some of them are letting go and merging into the ages."

"What do you mean?"

"Since the middle of the 16th century, they've spent every day, and every minute of every day, fighting a dreadful storm in one of the roughest places in the world."

She thought. "Yeah, that's certainly true," she nodded.

"They may just surrender and relax into the ultimate peace," he smiled. "Don't you think?"

"The only one I've talked to is Mac," she said. "The others just kind of stare at me when I try to speak to them.

"Yes," said Clint. "Same experience here."

"Then maybe they're shy, or…"

"Grieving?" he asked, and she nodded.

"Could we help them through it?"

"You mean, like end of life counseling?"

"I'm trying to think: what would it be like if we were suddenly transported 400 years into the past?" she asked. "How would we deal with it?"

"I'm trying to imagine," he shrugged. "Also, I wouldn't be married to you, which would be awful." He grinned and she hugged him.

"I don't think we have to worry about that for some time," she smiled. "Probably not for sixty or so years."

"Come on," said her husband. "Mickey got the hatch open."

They went down into the ship's hold. The place had been airing out, but a powerful stench of decay and wet permeated the old oak planking. "Where's the gold?" asked McKenna.

"They've moved it to a vault," said her husband. "Some bank not far from here." She nodded.

Anna walked to the end of the hold and listened to the sounds of the ancient ship.

"Mickey," she called. "Do you sense something down here?"

"No," he said. "But all my senses are so overloaded now I don't know what to say."

"Clint," Anna called. "Are you feeling anything?"

"Death, sorrow, anger, frustration," he said. "But no entity. No person, certainly not a demon."

Anna nodded. "I don't know what to say," she said. "I think the terror of 500 or so years is slow to depart." The others nodded. "Once the Captain died, the curse was lifted," Anna said.

"The passive tense," said McKenna. "So who lifted it?"

"I get the impression that whoever cursed the ship removed the curse when Van Zeeland died," said Anna.

"Yes," said Clint. "I feel that too. Or maybe the curse was never pronounced?"

"Is Van Zeeland dead for sure?" said McKenna.

Anna, Mickey and Clint paused and looked at each other. "Do you have any sense of him at all?" Anna asked the two men.

"No," they said.

"You don't either, right?" asked Mickey.

She shook her head. "But I do feel a malevolent presence on this ship."

The two men agreed. "I think it would be better if we burned it to the water line," she said. "A cursed ship, a cursed crew—"

"Let's get out of here," said McKenna. "Now."

"Wait," said a voice from up on top.

"Clovis," said McKenna. "What are you doing here?"

"I came to warn you," he said. "I can see it's a little late."

"What do you mean?" asked Anna.

"Over there," he said, pointing to a small door. Clovis came down the stairs and crossed to the door.

"It's all boarded up," noted Mickey, "except for that little door."

"Right," said Clovis. "But it's a worthless gesture. Behind that door is the reason the captain went aloft."

Anna, Mickey and Clint exchanged glances. McKenna said, "What is behind the door?"

"A monster, I think," said Clovis. "Mr. van Groningen, my father's friend, told me that the crew lived in fear of whatever the crew imprisoned in there."

"Good grief," said Anna.

"I know," said Clovis. "We mustn't open it."

They started up the ladder. A man stood at the top, waiting for them. He smiled.

"Welcome," he said. "I have met few Cymreigs in my life."

"Van Brandt," nodded McKenna.

Van Brandt stepped aside and let the group exit the stairway.

"Where are we?" asked Anna.

"At sea aboard *the Flying Dutchman*," said Brandt. "This is where I spent my existence—it's no good to call it a life, is it—for hundreds of years."

The sky had been blue and majestic over Cape Town, the temperature in the mid-60s. Now, however, the air was near zero, the waves were high.

"This isn't happening," said Mickey. "You're doing this in our minds." Van Brandt smiled and gave a little bow.

"I wanted you to see what my mini-eternity has looked like," said Van Brandt with a smirk.

"You also wanted to demonstrate your command of the Cymreig," said Anna. She slipped her hand into her husband's hand and put her arm around McKenna. "So, we're impressed. Thank you. Now please end this."

"All but one of you have the Cymreig," Van Brandt said. "Please understand and do nothing foolish. I am more powerful than all of you put together."

"Is that important to you?" asked Mickey. His tone was confident and chatty.

Van Brandt was a bit shaken that none of them seemed afraid. "I can demolish you with a thought," he said.

"Then take your best shot, as the cliché goes," said Clint. "We aren't afraid. We'll fight you, you can bet on it."

Anna, Clint and Mickey put McKenna behind them. The ship stopped swaying and heeling. The creaking stopped…

Brandt put his hands to his head. He looked, glared at something unseen, and shut his eyes in pain.

And vanished.

And once again they stood on the deck of an antique ship in dry dock.

"Where is he?" asked McKenna.

"I don't know," said Mickey. "He managed to stifle all three of us."

"But something happened to him," said Clint. "Something that hurt. A lot. He was in pain."

"That was me," said a voice from behind them.

They turned and found Therese. "Therese?" said McKenna. "You saved us?"

She shrugged. "I think so," she said. "Mom has been giving me lessons."

"So you do have the Cymreig?" asked Anna. "As Merlyn said?"

"Yes, I do," said Therese.

"But how. . ." asked McKenna.

"I don't know," said Therese. "Mom thinks Myrthynne might have interceded."

"He did?" asked Steve, coming into the room.

"I'm afraid so," said Clovis entering just behind Steve. An older man stood behind him. "I sensed it, but I didn't want to say anything."

Therese looked closely at the man behind Clovis.

"You were on *Der Fliegen Hollander*," she said.

"Yes," he said.

"Why?" she asked.

"It has to do with Brandt," said the man. "He's the one who called me to the ship."

"You mean he wanted to use you to escape?" asked Clint.

"Yes," said van Groningen.

"He's powerful," nodded Anna. "After all, he's had more than 400 years to perfect his use."

"More powerful than Myrthynne?" asked McKenna.

"I don't know," said her mother.

* * * * *

McKenna sat across from her husband in the dining hall, both of them nursing a late night glass of warm milk. "Is this situation getting any better?" she asked him.

"Frankly, my Dear," he said.

"Never mind," she sighed.

"Look, Mick," he said. "This adventure keeps getting more and more pathetic. We have a ship full of 500 year old seamen who want to go home, and we're not getting anything out of this. Why don't we just go and surf by Durban? Then, we'll go home. Okay?"

"No, not okay," she said. "Therese is an old and dear friend, and she's dealing with something none of us understand."

"How are we supposed to help?" he argued. "I don't want to fight a Cymreig. Yeah, we can do some stuff, but not enough to get past him. I sensed how powerful he is and he can absolutely demolish all of us with a thought."

"Even Mom? Gayle?" asked his wife.

"I think so," he said. "Mickey and I talked it over and we agreed. We're afraid of him."

"You four have the Cymreig too, don't you? And Clovis too?"

"Yeah, but not like him," Clint said.

"Okay, but let's think it over," she said. "Why not just give the gold to the survivors and beat it then?"

He considered. "Because I'm not sure anyone is going to survive," he said. "We only have a dozen crewmen from the ship left."

"What's happening to them?"

"I think they're overwhelmed with despair," he said. "And nothing we say to them is any help, at all."

"What do you mean?"

"They've been living the same day over and over for four hundred some years," he smiled. "They didn't know it was happening. Every day the same thing happened, they went to sleep, then their memories re-booted. What kept them going was an appalling fear of not seeing their loved ones or their homes, even their country again."

She thought. "Why are some of them disappearing?"

"Despair," he said. "It destroys all men who cannot escape from it. They stop living."

"I can't imagine it," she said.

"Depression can be inherited," he said. "You know that."

"I remember one man with whom I worked. He told me that he'd go out the front door in the morning and see nothing but blackness," she nodded. "But that's extreme. Most people with depression don't get that bad. Still, for the people who suffer with it, they have a mental anchor all day, holding them back, dragging them down."

"So you think the crew is giving up?" asked Clint.

"Yeah, I do," she said. "They see nothing worth living for in this century, at this time. They'd never catch up enough to live normal lives no matter how much training they received."

"Yeah," he said. "That sure sounds depressing."

"I don't think even the Cymreig can help."

"Probably not," he agreed. "I mean, I can do some teaching with it, and I can ease their minds—well, we all can—but we can't get them to live in this world."

At that moment the other Cymreigs came in. Anna Fixx sat across the table from Clint. "Do you think the situation is under control?" she asked her son-in-law.

"How many crew men are left?" asked Clint.

"Ten or twelve, I think," said Mickey.

Gayle nodded. "I've been trying to talk to them," she said. "I sense a terrible depression."

"Yeah," said McKenna. She summarized the conversation she and her husband had been having.

"One of the remaining crewmen told me that their friends say goodbye, shake hands, and then just…er…vanish." Gayle shuddered. "Clothes, bodies, jewelry, personal effects—all of it just disappears. Time catches up to everything, those things fall in on themselves, and in seconds nothing is left."

"What about Mac?" asked McKenna.

Mickey shook his head. "I think he's struggling to make sense of what he's done," he said. "He's coming to understand life at all costs is too high a price."

"I think I understand," said McKenna. "He got sick of routine. He's a person who doesn't like to do the same thing over and over."

"Yeah," said Mickey. "I had a student one time who had a job at an office. Her job was the same thing every day. Filing; then typing; then all the other things at an office. Nothing varied much from day to day. She loved it."

"I'd hate it," asserted McKenna. "I deplore routine." Several heads nodded. "I don't think it's a matter of intelligence. Rather it's the way she was hard wired."

"And Mac is the opposite of that student, that's what you're saying?" said Gayle. McKenna nodded.

"Yeah," she said. "He couldn't deal with the same routine over and over, scrubbing the same ten square feet of the deck, going into the rigging, and so on. He needs to have challenges, variations in routine, something new all the time."

"So what do we do?" asked Gayle.

"I think we should get him going on a project, like organizing a memorial for the *Hollander* and its crew," said Therese.

Clint and McKenna looked at one another. He shrugged. "I don't know," he said. "He's bought himself some time, I guess, in a fine body. But that body is 400 years old. How long it'll last I can't say. We need to ask about his personal health all the time. Also to keep an eye on those remaining men."

"How about letting him set up a trust for the descendants of the Dutchman?" said Steve. "Just spitballing. I don't know that they could be found."

"Here's an idea," said Gayle. "Let's ask him what he wants to do."

They found Mac sitting on the front deck of *Arcturus*. He smiled at them, remarked that it was a gorgeous day, and he had a towel around his neck, running shoes on his feet and sweat soaking his tee shirt.

He smiled. "I just took a run," he said. "This new body is terrific. It isn't used to running, of course, but I think I can get in shape in no time."

"How old are you, Dad?" asked Therese.

"I think about 35," he smiled. "I have that sense anyway."

"Dad," said Therese. "How many sailors are left?"

"I don't know," he replied. "Less than came aboard. I'm sad about that. They don't seem to feel it's worth living if they have to live somewhere apart from the world they know."

"Can we help?" asked Therese.

He thought. "Maybe," he said, drawing out the word. "They need to see some of the world as it has become. If they can put it in perspective, so much the better. I think they really need to talk to someone also. I don't speak Dutch, though I can get by in Afrikaans, like you, Therese."

"I can try to work with them," she said. "I think we need a priest, though."

"A priest?" he asked. "What was happening with the Church in Holland at the time they disappeared?"

"They're probably Protestant Reformed," shrugged Therese. "But I'll ask."

Therese and McKenna decided to go to the gym on the South African Coast Guard Cutter. They found Anna, Casey, Rand and Mickey talking with Clint in the galley before they reached the gym, however.

"What's happening?" asked Therese.

The Cymreigs exchanged glances. "The crew men keep disappearing," said Anna. "One disappeared a few moments ago. It sort of shook us up, I must say."

"What did Dad say?" asked Therese.

"He kind of shrugged," said Clint. "Like it doesn't bother him much."

"Hmm," said Steve. "Yeah, it might not. Remember, he spent his life bowling over people. To change his mind and his approach is slow in coming."

Gayle sat down with a cup of coffee. "I think we need to get out of here, Steve."

Steve did a double take. "But why?" he asked. "This port

seems pleasant and the entire area around Cape Town is gorgeous."

"Something's wrong," said Gayle. "I sense it. And I can't figure why you guys haven't."

Mickey exchanged glances with Anna and Clint. "Do you feel something wrong?" he said.

"I haven't," said Anna.

"Me neither," said Clint. "I think we're all disturbed about the disappearances of crewmen—" the others nodded—"but I haven't sensed anything wrong."

"Where is that Cymreig we faced?" asked Anna.

"I don't know," said Mickey. "We haven't seen him since we met him on the Dutchman, have we?"

The others shook their heads.

"So where is he?" Anna asked. "Has he vanished too?"

"I don't think I ever saw him down there with the others," said Mickey.

"I don't remember him either," said the others.

CHAPTER TWENTY-EIGHT

A week later, Therese and McKenna sat on the back deck of *Arcturus*, looking at the work going on across the way on *The Flying Dutchman*. McKenna brought the conversation around to the end of the adventure. "Look, Therese," she said. "Clint and I are ready to go home, unless you need us."

"I'm sorry for holding you up," said her friend. "I have so appreciated having you here."

"I think you're going to need to go back to work, aren't you?"

"Yes, probably," said her friend. "Though the bullion we recovered seems to be ours, now."

"Have we lost more seamen?" said McKenna.

"My dad—Oosterhuis—is soon going to be the only one left," nodded Therese.

"I'm sorry," said McKenna. "They should have gotten more out of life. It doesn't seem fair."

"They've made their decisions," said Therese. "The riches meant nothing to them."

Gayle came in and sat with them. "Beautiful day in Cape Town," she said. "Aren't you two going to go out and about?"

"I want to make sure everything is okay here," said Therese.

"Is there something you can do about it if it isn't okay?"

asked her mother.

"I don't know," said Therese. "I just don't like to abandon my post, if you know what I mean."

"Nonsense," said her mother. "Go and do something, the four of you. I'll hang around."

McKenna and Therese grabbed their husbands and headed off to lunch at a seafood place.

"Did we lose any more of the men from the *Dutchman*?" Therese asked Steve.

"Well, not today," said Steve. "Your Dad—or Oosterhuis, whatever he is—is working with the stragglers. But I sense real depression."

"They're angry," said Clint. "I guess I don't blame them. They have no frame of reference whatever for this time, they have more than four centuries of nightmares to contend with. They know that everyone they knew back home is gone and their world has long since passed them by."

"Isn't Depression mostly anger?" Steve asked McKenna, who shrugged and gave a nod. "These guys have a right to be angry. We've offered to take them back to Holland, but most of them are indifferent about it. They seem to have no interest, even in the least."

"Yeah," said McKenna. "So what can we do to help?"

"Teach them," said Clint. "Teach them to read and write and understand what's happened since the *Hollander* vanished. Teach them to live on their own, to adjust to this situation."

"That won't be easy," said McKenna.

"No, I know that," said Clint. "They have no or little education, and they don't know what their future holds. They need something to live for."

They heard the sirens in the background but didn't pay much attention to them. Then Steve came alert. "Those sirens," he said. "They're coming from the harbor."

All four heads jerked in the direction of the harbor. Then they exchanged glances. Steve and Clint threw some money on the table and the four friends began to run to the harbor.

* * * * *

The Flying Dutchman, ancient timbers as dry as chalk dust, stood ablaze in the Cape Town Harbor. Harbor fire boats and land based fire engines sprayed water on the antique vessel.

"My Gosh," said McKenna. "Wouldn't it be ironic if this thing survives for centuries packed in ice, only to burn to the water line within a few weeks of escaping."

"It'll be okay, Mick," said Therese. "They struck the fire. Looks like minimal damage. Still…" her voice faded away and she became lost in thought.

"What's up, Honey?" said her husband.

"Clint, don't you think it's strange that the *Dutchman* caught fire?" said McKenna.

"I see what you mean," said Steve. "Why would it wait until now? When the four of us are gone?"

"Maybe you're making too much of it, huh?" suggested Clint.

"Possible," said Steve. He didn't look convinced.

"You think this thing was cursed?" asked Therese with a smile.

"Well, the important things have been removed," said Clint. "The people, the gold, any artifacts that have any value were transported off the ship. This is just antique oak and cloth and rope."

"But we could have studied it," said Therese. "Think of what we could have learned."

"Like what?" said Steve. "I don't think anything on that ship would move our knowledge of seamanship along, or that would teach us about the past, can you?"

"I tend to agree with Steve," said Clint. "Remember Mr. Potter in the Building and Loan after George's father dies? He talks about what he calls 'Sentimental Hogwash.'"

"*It's a Wonderful Life*," grinned Therese. "You unfeeling louts. You have no sensitivity."

Steve chuckled. "The good news is that no one was aboard to get hurt. *The Dutchman* isn't worth anything. And look at the real Oosterhuis. He was willing to undergo extreme pain and suffering with cancer to get off of the thing."

"Hmm," mused Clint. "But why did this thing catch fire? It seems strange that this would happen so soon after coming to port. Was there something on board that we weren't supposed to see?"

"Like what?" asked McKenna.

"I don't know," he asked. "But we got a significant threat from the resident Cymreig, and I can't imagine why he'd want to hold us back from uncovering the truth about this ship."

"The truth?" asked Therese.

"Well, yes," said Clint. "This ship was hidden for centuries, lost in the polar ice cap. It came to light only because we went after your father, Therese. Someone—perhaps that rogue Cymreig—has tried to keep us from exploring the ship, from going after what the truth of the ship was."

"There was a truth?" asked Steve.

"I think so, yes," said Clint. "Someone went to a lot of

trouble to try to keep us from recovering the ship. Why would he do that? And now, why would he want to burn the ship to the water line?"

McKenna bit her lip. "Okay, if what you're saying is valid—" she began.

"Me? Say something valid? That's quite a long shot, isn't it?" grinned Clint.

She whacked his arm. "How many crewmen are left?" she asked.

"I think ten still. These guys seem to be responding to Mac," said Steve.

"This surprises you?" asked Clint. "I mean, you didn't have much good to say about him before we recovered him."

"It's true," admitted Steve. "He doesn't walk, or talk, or do much of anything the way the old Mac would."

"Do you know what made the difference?" asked McKenna.

Her best friend spoke up. "I think it was the ghastly hard work and danger on the *Dutchman*. He saw how hard the men worked, the sort of life they had, the dreary monotony and danger that always lingered in the background."

"What do you think, Steve?" asked McKenna.

"I don't know," he said. "I think Therese has a point. When he saw what the life of a laborer consisted of, it seems to have worked in a powerful way on him."

"But he had a tough job in college," said Therese. "He worked as a laborer at a steel mill in the summer. He made his money for college in the summers and sometimes during winter break, too. He knew that business pretty well, at least in the Melt Shop."

"The Melt Shop?" said McKenna.

"That's where they make the steel," said Therese. "I mean, they operate the furnaces where they melt down the ore and the scrap metal and like that."

"Right," said McKenna. "It sounds like it would be Hell in the summer."

"It was," said Mac McNulty, who came into the galley and poured himself a cup of coffee. "On the other hand it convinced me to finish my education and learn how to run a business rather than be subject to a bawling, red-faced thug of a supervisor."

"How so?" asked Clint.

"When I worked there the first summer, I picked up a piece of slag," said Mac. "I took it home with me. Every time I didn't feel like studying, I'd heft that rock for a while and think about spending my life in the Melt Shop. Pretty good motivator."

"I guess so," muttered McKenna.

"Lots of summer jobs do that, I think," said Steve. "Mr. McNulty—" he began.

"Mac, please, Steve," said Mac with a smile. "You're my son now."

Steve smiled and nodded thanks. "I wanted to ask how many of the sailors are left," Steve went on.

Mac's smile continued. "We haven't lost any today," he said. "We still have ten of them. I'm hopeful we can keep them around."

"Dad—" said Therese, her voice tentative.

"Uh huh?" he said.

"We have a lot of problems here," she said. "And I don't know how to handle them. What are we going to do? The McNulty empire is about to crumble."

Mac was silent for a time. He pulled out a chair and sat down.

"Therese, I have been thinking about that," he said. "I think it may be time to break up the group, sell off the assets, and get out of things."

"You would want to dissolve the business?" gasped Therese. Mac nodded. "But Dad, this was your whole life…"

"I know," he said. "But I didn't have any life until I went aboard the *Dutchman*. Now I have something to live for, not just money."

"What's that?" asked Steve.

"Well, freedom for one," said Mac. "Peace and rest, for another."

"Don't forget love," said Therese, and her sarcasm went over the head of her father.

"You're right," he said, not without sincerity. "I've never really allowed myself to experience love. I need to do that. I don't much like living alone, and relationships with young women haven't stirred me much."

"You want to go back to Mom?" asked Therese.

"I've been thinking about it," said Mac. "I doubt that she'd have me, though."

"You could ask," shrugged Steve. "I can see she still loves you. Perhaps with some counseling…"

"Well, we're a long way from that," said Mac. "But I'll consider it."

"What about the Cymreig?" asked Clint.

"The what?" asked Mac.

"We—that is, those of us with the red hair and green eyes— have the ancient gift called the Cymreig," Clint started.

"Of course," said Mac. "I wouldn't say I know all about it. Still, remember that I was married to Gayle for quite a while, and I saw some of what she can do."

"Yes, but there's something else," said Therese. "We've had an encounter with someone from the *Dutchman* who has the Cymreig."

Mac blinked. He started to speak, then closed his mouth. His surprise was evident. "How is that possible?" he asked. "Isn't the Cymreig only found in the Irish descendants of Faerae?"

"Well, we thought so," said Clint. "I'd never heard of a Dutch Cymreig."

"All he can do is help us, right?" asked Mac.

"I don't think so," said Clint. "Anna, Mickey and I all sensed evil about him."

"Is it possible he isn't a Cymreig?" asked Mac.

"He seems to be earthbound, a sinister type of spirit," said Clint. "I don't know what he is. None of us do. I don't sense him among the survivors."

"Is he dangerous?" asked Mac.

"Yes," said Clint. "He's more than dangerous. He has far more ability with the Cymreig than any of us do."

"Where is he?" asked Mac.

"We don't know," said Clint. "We have no sense of him now. But he has shown up several times without warning. He's brought us terrible visions, threats and that."

"Do you know what he wants?" Mac asked.

"No," said Clint. "No, we can't imagine. But he has chosen not to step into the Light with his shipmates."

Mac considered. "Why don't you get out of here while you're safe?" he asked the friends.

"We're concerned," said McKenna. "We intended to find the Dutchman to help you, to bring you home, but we may have unleashed far more than we bargained for."

"Wait a minute," said Therese. "Is it possible…" she stopped and bit her lip.

"What?" asked Mac.

"What if everyone has been wrong about the *Dutchman* all these years?" asked Therese.

"What do you mean?" asked Steve.

"What if the Captain did something to keep a monster from being released on society?" Therese managed.

"You mean, the Cymreig on the ship?" said Clint.

"Yes," said Therese. "Look, McKenna, didn't you say that you guys had never heard of a Dutch Cymreig?"

"Yeah, that's true," said McKenna, and Clint nodded.

"So what was this guy doing in Holland?" Therese asked.

"Hmm," nodded Clint, taking her point. "Of course, his abilities may not have been any more extraordinary than ours when he shipped aboard. He could have hidden who he was without difficulty. I know, because I used to do it all the time so people wouldn't think I was weird. Then, when he sees the gold, and the riches, he decides to take advantage of his ability, displace the captain, take the ship and the gold for himself."

"So you think the Captain went aloft and—" said McKenna.

"—And prayed," said her best friend. "Prayed that God would deliver them from the curse of the Cymreig. Brandt must have begun to work on the members of the crew, to influence them to mutiny, even. Will it pass?"

Mac had been silent. "No, that can't be right," he said. "I was on the ship for several days. Each day, the captain ascended to the top mast and screamed at God: horrible profanity, curses, vile denunciations…"

"Did he scream?" asked McKenna. "And could you hear it?"

"Well, no," said McNulty after a few moments. "I could hear him screaming, but I don't know what the words really were. People always have said it was vulgar blasphemy, but now that I think, I don't know."

"Then what about the possibility that he was screaming to overcome the wind?" asked McKenna. "And what he was screaming was a prayer?"

McNulty was silent. "And because of his prayer, the ship became sealed into eternity."

"So any ship that comes into contact with the Dutchman was cursed and ultimately sank rather than let an evil Cymreig loose?" asked Therese.

"That's where the legends came from," said Clint.

"So why did we survive?" asked Therese.

"I think we were shielded to some extent," said Clint. "After all, several of us—Gayle, Anna, Mickey, Therese and me—are also Cymreigs. Not only that, but we can sense when someone is trying to harm us, and we have some defenses that go up."

"So this may be more serious than it originally seemed," said McKenna.

"What do you mean?" asked Clint.

McKenna turned to Mac. "Mr. McNulty," she said, "Did you hear what the Captain screamed at heaven?"

"Well, no, I didn't," admitted Mac.

"What if he went aloft every day to pray that the Cymreig could be conquered?" McKenna asked. "What if he maintained the curse in an effort to keep the Cymreig from being unleashed on the world?"

Silence descended. "This is possible?" Therese asked her father.

"I never had much of a chance to talk to the Captain," said Mac. "I didn't get to know any of the men, either, because no one knew me from day to day, do you see?"

"I think so," said Steve. "They thought you were their shipmate, and they really didn't have time to develop a relationship, what with the storm and all."

"Right," said Mac. "I also don't think Oosterhuis was especially well liked, either. The other sailors tended to avoid conversation with me. I always felt they were afraid of me, as well."

"You mean they were afraid of Oosterhuis, right?" asked Clint.

"Yes," said Mac. "Evidently he was not popular with the others on the ship. Even now, when I talk to the survivors, there's a hesitation, a reluctance to engage with me."

"Because of Oosterhuis," said Steve.

"Exactly," said Therese, looking serious.

Mac sat down and considered. "Then all we have to do is let the men perish in the normal way," he said.

"But what about the Cymreig?" asked McKenna. "I gather that we've set him loose on society at large. Can we get him back?"

"I just don't know," admitted Clint. "Remember, none of us have ever heard of an evil Cymreig."

"Could his evil nature be the reason he went to Holland?" asked Therese.

"What do you mean?" asked McKenna.

"What if the Irish Cymreigs drove him out, so that he escaped to Holland?" asked Therese. "We've never heard any stories about it, but could they have thought they were safe?"

"You mean, with him gone, they didn't worry about things," nodded Clint.

"I do have to say," said Steve, "that the legend of The Dutchman never quite made sense."

"How do you mean?" asked McKenna.

"I know about the evil of pirates, like Henry Morgan, or Blackbeard, or any one of several others," said Steve.

"Right," said McKenna. "My mom used to tell me stories of Blackbeard. Legends say that one night, he called his officers into his cabin, bolted the doors and windows, and lit a pot of sulfur. Of course, the men were close to suffocation in seconds. Blackbeard, according to the legend, gave every evidence of liking it. He told the men that they'd died, and that they were in Hell, and were just now meeting up. He told them they'd better get used to it, because they'd be breathing brimstone smoke for all eternity."

"Good grief," said Therese. "Why didn't the crew mutiny?"

"No mutiny is recorded, as far as I know," said McKenna. "He reigned over the ship with not just an iron hand, but with a red hot glowing iron hand. If they crossed him he wouldn't hesitate to throw men overboard, or do something worse to them."

"He must have been a pretty terrible person," agreed Clint.

"Ugh," agreed Therese. "That sounds like an understatement."

"Well, yes," said Steve. "But what if that's what the crew of the Dutchman had to deal with?"

"They wouldn't want to release that terror on any society," said McKenna. "And they really couldn't defeat a powerful Cymreig. They may have thought that the bravest and most paramount thing to do was to surrender the ship for all eternity."

"I wonder why they didn't just pray for death," said Therese. "Or why they didn't just sink the ship."

"I think they feared that the Cymreig might escape," said McKenna.

Silence fell on the group. "You mean that when we found the ship, we unleashed a terror on the world," said Steve.

"Yes, I do mean that," said McKenna. "I don't know how we could get that terror back under control."

* * * * *

Gayle stepped out of a shower and dried in the luxuriant towels provided in the master suite of *Arcturus*. She slipped into a light silk robe and sat at the small desk that served as a dressing table for the stateroom.

Lost in thought, as she had been for days, it seemed, she brushed out her luxuriant copper hair and stared at herself in the mirror. She still had a little guilt at being in the main bedroom. Gayle had moved into the master cabin on the vessel, not because she'd wanted to, but because her daughter had insisted.

"It's yours, Mom," said Therese. "It's really yours. You are the only person Dad has ever loved, and if he was in his right mind, he'd insist that you take it."

Gayle had quibbled for a bit, and offered it to her daughter and her new husband, then to McKenna and Clint, but none of them would hear of it. Phooey, she thought, and acquiesced.

She certainly had gotten more than she counted on when she

married Mac. She'd gone to twelve years of pariochial elementary and high school, where she'd distinguished herself with her classroom efforts. Then she had stayed home for the first two years of college, attending a community college. She again attained superb grades, outstanding recommendations and honors that accompanied her associate of arts degree.

She transferred to the same college that Mac attended, and kept to herself, rarely dating or going to campus events. She'd met Mac at a football dance in her second year at the college. Walking back from the stadium, where she saw another college team crush the University team, she stopped with her roommate at a fraternity open house. A loud band performed rock music in front of the house, and the fraternity was serving punch, a poor attempt at finger sandwiches and potato chips.

As Gayle stood at the outside of the crowd, watching her roommate dance and have fun, a man came over to her and said hello.

"Hello," she responded, not looking him in the eye.

"My name is Mac," he said, and extended his hand. She took it and identified herself also. Standard conversation ensued: where do you live, what's your major, what year in school are you, where are you from, and so on. She smiled and even began to relax as they chatted.

The band concluded and began to pack up, and Gayle's roomie came over to say she'd met someone who had invited her to have dinner with him. Gayle nodded and said she'd see her back at the dorm.

"Why don't you and I go for a bite to eat?" asked Mac. "I know a great place for burgers. I promise it'd be better than these lousy sandwiches, anyhow." Gayle laughed and smiled and said okay.

Their first date had lasted until almost two in the morning. They had breakfast the next morning at her dorm, and then spent the day together.

Within a month, their friends began to realize that something significant had happened between Gayle and Mac McNulty. They married a week after graduation. Therese was born eleven months later.

Gayle, sitting in front of the mirror and putting on cold cream to remove her minimal makeup, smiled to think about the first five years of their marriage. It hadn't been something out of the gift of the Magi, to be sure—Mac made a great deal of money almost from the beginning. They had tried for years to produce a sibling for Therese, but to no avail.

She let her mind skip through the divorce, as she always did. It certainly had not been what she wanted by any means. Mac, however, had been determined and the most painful year of her life left her alone and rich, with a brilliant child; a comfortable, beautiful home; and a broken heart.

She watched Mac from a distance, talking to him when necessary, focusing on her daughter—her talented, beautiful daughter—and watching her develop into the exceptional woman Gayle knew she could be.

Gayle winced as she considered what her life had been like. Alone, shy, withdrawn, she'd been portrayed as some sort of sex bombshell in the tabloid media. They appeared to delight in linking her in romance with people she'd never even met. She would see pictures of herself on newsstands in cheap scandal sheets posed on the arm of some actor, or pro golfer, or politician, people whom she'd never met, and with whom she'd never ever considered a romantic relationship.

Still, she had managed to keep the media away from Therese, protected her, loved her and always tried to make her feel safe. This marriage to Steve answered her prayers for her daughter. She knew Steve as a man without guile, moral, courageous and devoted. Gayle began to get excited to think about grandchildren, Christmases, birthdays—

Someone knocked at her door. Puzzled, Gayle pulled her robe together and knotted it as she walked to the door.

"Mac," she said, puzzled to see him at the door.

"Gayle," he said. "Can I please come in?"

"Why?" she asked.

"I'm terrified," said Mac/Oosterhuis, and his distress was visible.

"I'm sorry you are," said Gayle, trying not to encourage him, keeping her tone calm and neutral. "But I can't help."

"Haven't I always come to you when I'm afraid?" he asked.

"It doesn't matter," she said. "We are not married any more. For you to come into my bedroom would not only be inappropriate but a terrible example. You need a priest, perhaps a psychiatrist, or maybe both, but not an ex-wife."

He thought for a few moments, looking her up and down. Gayle pulled the robe closed even more. "Okay," he said. "Then we'll do it the other way." Before Gayle could react, he stepped forward and seized her. He worked hard to kiss her, holding her neck with one hand and tearing away her robe with the other.

Gayle was terrified, now. He wrestled her to the bed, stopping her screams with his kisses, untying the sash on the robe.

"Mac," she said. "Mac, no. This is rape. Stop it now."

He didn't respond. He had her on the bed in a moment, and

his own clothes came away as he pinned her to the bed. Then he forced himself on her, painful and unwelcome. Gayle tried to reach out with the Cymreig, but she couldn't penetrate his defenses against it—

In an abrupt moment of insight, she got it. She knew who this was.

This man was not Mac. He was being crude in his outrageous presumption, his vulgar language, and in his violent thrusting at her. He pinned her to the bed, oblivious to her discomfort and rising anger.

The pain eased in a few moments and Gayle forced herself to groan as if enjoying the interlude. He smiled, making clear that he relished every second.

Gayle stretched her arms up and embraced him around the neck. She was right: he appeared to enjoy it. She bent her arms at the elbow and undid the clasp on the necklace. He didn't notice. Indeed, he increased the speed and concentrated.

In a moment he moaned with pleasure and shut his eyes to appreciate the experience and the power of a long suppressed orgasm took him. Gayle saw her opportunity. She fastened the clasp behind his neck.

Almost at once the man understood that something had changed. He gasped as if she'd wrapped a red-hot chain around him. He jerked up and scrambled backward across the bed and to the floor. He tried to pull at the chain, but every time he touched it, he cried out with pain.

She heard the banging at the door and rose quickly, pulling her robe shut. She crossed to the door and jerked it open. Mac stood there as if in shock, looking first at her and then at the naked man struggling in pain on the ground.

"What's wrong with him?" he cried.

"My cross," she said. "I fastened it around his neck. It's burning him."

Now Steve and Clint ran in. "What…" began Steve, then saw his mother-in-law's face and knew.

"Be quick," commanded Mac, and the three men hoisted the moaning Cymreig and hurried down the hall. Now McKenna and Therese joined the group. McKenna threw open the door to the deck and the men hurried through, dragging the struggling poseur along.

Now Clovis and Van Doren ran out and joined the group. "Oosterhuis!" cried the older man in amazement. "But I thought---"

"Stand him up straight," commanded Mac. As they did, Mac stepped behind Brandt, wrapped his arms below the man's chest and jerked. The Cymreig exhaled with violence as Mac took a deep breath and plunged the two of them over the railing into the dark water.

"What's he doing?" cried Therese.

"I think I know," said Steve. "It's okay."

Mac and the Cymreig vanished into the deep water. Thirty seconds went by. A minute. "Daddy?" cried Therese. But nothing happened.

Another few seconds went by before they saw a ripple and Mac's head broke the surface. Gayle ran to the diving platform with Steve and Clint right behind. Clint launched himself into a racing dive, and hit the water ten feet from Mac, who seemed to be near unconsciousness in the frigid water.

Clint seized Mac, and wrapped his right arm around Mac from his right shoulder to his left armpit. Then he began sidestroking back to the platform as Mac choked and gasped.

Steve and Therese pulled and tugged at Mac and got him up onto the platform as Clint climbed up the ladder. McKenna wrapped a towel around her husband's shoulder.

"Brandy and Water?" she grinned.

"No water," he managed with a straight face and they laughed together a little.

"Any sign of Brandt?" asked Mac, teeth chattering a little.

"No," said Therese. "What happened?"

"The cross," he said. "Brandt was nearly helpless to do anything about it and having it around his neck weakened him. He couldn't use the Cymreig to vanish or help himself in any way. So when I jerked all the air out of his lungs, he couldn't grab a breath. I let us sink down to twenty feet or so and loosened my grip."

"So of course he inhaled the seawater," said McKenna. "He didn't have a choice."

Mac nodded. "I grabbed him in a full nelson wrestling hold until he went limp, and unconscious, but he died pretty fast. I'm sorry, Honey," he said, turning to Gayle. "I couldn't retrieve your cross. He…"

Gayle embraced him. "I don't mind," she said. "I can find another." To everyone's surprise, she kissed her ex-husband, long and with exceptional devotion. As they backed away, Therese wrapped a blanket around her mother's shoulders. Then she embraced her mother and father. Steve walked forward to join the group.

"Come on," said McKenna, and she and her husband made their way up the stairs. Mickey and Anna met them with hot coffee and blankets. The Fixxes and the Logans sat at a deck table while Clint took a hot shower and changed.

* * * * *

McKenna and Clint sat on the rear deck of *Arcturus*, enjoying coffee and a couple of rolls with some butter. They chatted in hushed tones about what had transpired the night before.

"Are Gayle and Mac okay?" she asked.

Clint affected a Scottish accent. "I truly dinna know," he said. "They seem to be, and I don't sense any violence in the atmosphere around the ship."

"Do you think that Gayle and Mac might reconcile?"

"Well, it seems possible now," he nodded. "I know she was earnest in hugging him last night."

"He appears to be a man who has never grown up," Clint said. "He's still in Peter Pan mode: security based in money, in possessions, in flying away from responsibility in a marriage…"

"Nicely said," she agreed. "But when their lives were on the line, he came through for her, didn't he?"

"So, will they reconcile?"

"Anyone's guess, I suppose," smiled McKenna. "I think they both needed to grow up."

Therese came out and sat at the table with them. She poured herself some coffee and smiled at her friends.

"When are you going home?" she asked.

"No rush," said McKenna. "What did you have in mind?"

"Would you like to sail *Arcturus* with Steve and me?"

Clint and McKenna looked at one another, mouths open and eyebrows raised. "What on earth?"

"Dad promoted me," she said. "I'm going to New York and take over the hospitality wing of the company at corporate headquarters. He's going to start doing a bunch of divesting, and I think he and Mom will retire. I think he wants me to run the whole show in time."

"Makes sense," said Clint. "Who would be better than you?"

Therese shrugged. "I don't know if I want all that, though," she said. "I'm starting to think that I'd prefer having kids, living in a suburb, maybe homeschooling, and having a normal life. I kind of like the idea of being a mom."

McKenna grinned. "Well, maybe our kids can be friends," she said.

Therese stared at her friends. Then she blinked and smiled. "You mean, you're…uh…"

"Yeah, I do," said McKenna. The two best friends hugged as Steve joined the group.

"She told you?" said Steve.

"Well, yeah, if you mean we should go home with you on *Arcturus*," said Clint.

Steve embraced his wife. "So?"

"So, when do we leave?" asked Clint.

"Well, we do have to get Gayle to the Doctor this morning," said Steve.

"Is she sick?" cried McKenna.

"No," smiled Therese. "Pregnant."

Therese grinned at McKenna and Clint as they struggled for words. "You mean, Brandt?"

"Yes, Brandt," said Therese. "And it seems pretty likely that the baby will be a Cymreig."

McKenna considered. "So we could have another friend for the play group?"

Therese nodded. "She's sure," she said. "I'm afraid Brandt succeeded in his assault on her, and she sensed the Cymreig in the baby."

"Oh, brother," said Clint. "Another Cymreig?" McKenna and Therese whacked him.

"Anna, and Mickey too, are pretty sure," said Therese. "Anna told me that she was aware within minutes when you were conceived."

"I remember," said McKenna. "She told me."

"What about you?" said Steve, with a broad grin at McKenna.

"I don't have any sense of my baby," said McKenna. "But then I don't have the Cymreig, either. The baby? I guess we'll wait and see."

"It's going to be a fun group," said Therese. "Your Mom and Dad, Mickey and Karen—they're all eager to cruise home with us."

"What about the crewmen?" said Clint.

"Three or four are left," said Steve. "I'm thinking we'll take them with us. Getting back to sea, breathing sea air—I'll think they'll feel at home more there. I'm thinking we'll cruise the African west coast, and make our way to Holland. They'll be welcomed as heroes, I'm pretty sure."

"Have you talked to them about it?" asked Therese.

"Mac did," he said. "I think it might work. Mac said they seemed to like the idea. So he's taking them shopping, getting them clothing, shaving gear, shoes, and so on. He can work with them on public speaking, all that. "

"When can we leave?" asked Clint.

"How about a week?" said Therese.

"Make it two," said McKenna. "Clint and I want to go surfing near Durban."

¬ THE END¬

Title: ACID

- Author: Jeff Lovell
- Publisher: TotalRecall Publications, Inc.
- HARD COVER ISBN: 978-1-59095-116-3
- PAPERBACK, ISBN: 978-1-59095-117-0
- EBOOK, Nook, Kindle, ISBN: 978-1-59095-118-7
- Number of pages: 352
- Publication Date: 2013

Rick Howell, living in the shadow of two women who have the power to change reality, must risk his life to stop the genocidal exploits of a desperate lunatic who wants to acquire their powers. The discovery of a mind controlling drug opens a pathway to frightening mental abilities for Rachel Farrell, who can move backward and forward in time at will, while Donna Riske, Rachel's best friend, can control the thoughts of others.

Title: The Coven of the Spring

- Author: Jeff Lovell
- Publisher: TotalRecall Publications, Inc.
- HARD COVER ISBN: 978-1-59095-113-2
- PAPERBACK, ISBN: 978-1-59095-114-9
- EBOOK, Nook, Kindle, ISBN: 978-1-59095-115-6
- Number of pages: 336
- Publication Date: 2013

An ancient secret, with frightening new powers, emerges to terrify and destroy.

Grace DeRosa, a gifted research chemist, lives with her husband Jim and their seventeen year old daughter Crissy. Grace finds a hidden spring in the woods near Salem, Massachusetts. She discovers that the consumed water imparts unique and fearful powers that lead to the ability to read minds, create terrifying mental pictures and force the user's will on others.

Title: Emerald

- Author: Jeff Lovell
- Publisher: TotalRecall Publications, Inc.
- HARD COVER ISBN: 9781590950807
- PAPERBACK, ISBN: 9781590950814
- EBOOK, ISBN: 9781590950821
- Number of pages: 348
- Publication Date: 2015

Emerald begins with a pirate assault on a merchant vessel. Blackbeard, or Edward Teach, terrorized the east coast of America from Nova Scotia down to the Virgin Islands. This book shows how people with a unique mental power called the Knack fight against the evil of pirates from 1715 to the present day, and even includes a long look at the court of King Arthur, and his chief advisor Myrthynne, who also had the most powerful manifestation of the Knack. This book, then, flows in several time periods and pulls together romance, villainy and a dramatic treasure, all of which frame a love story between a woman with the Knack and a man devoted to loving and protecting her.

Title: The Cape

- Author: Jeff Lovell
- Publisher: TotalRecall Publications, Inc.
- HARD COVER, ISBN: 9781590952078
- PAPERBACK, ISBN: 9781590952085
- EBOOK, ISBN: 9781590952092
- Number of pages: 228
- Publication Date: 2016

People say that *Der Fleigen Hollander—The Flying Dutchman*, as it is known in English—vanished with all hands in the sixteenth century off the Cape of Good Hope. Yet the ship has been by reliable, truthful people all over the world, suggesting that the ship is trapped in a time warp somewhere in the treacherous ocean south of the Cape. When her father is kidnapped by the ship, Therese goes to find him and rescue him from the self-imposed, Purgatorial imprisonment. In the search she is joined by her mother and a lifetime best friend, who seek to help Therese draw his soul back from the pit of Hell before he is lost for all eternity.

Title: The Ghost Of White Island

- Author: Jeff Lovell
- Publisher: TotalRecall Publications, Inc.
- HARD COVER ISBN: 9781590951194
- PAPERBACK, ISBN: 9781590952092
- EBOOK, Nook, Kindle, ISBN: 9781590952092
- Number of pages: 348
- Publication Date: 2015

In 1715, a ship's carpenter tried to rape the 14 year old daughter of the captain of a British warship and was flogged almost to death. He mutinied and captured the ship, killing the captain and forcing his daughter into marriage. After falling in with Blackbeard, he abandoned his young wife on a cold, bitter rock called White Island, off the coast of New Hampshire. When he was caught and hanged by the British Navy, his treasure vanished into history. Many people believe that Martha, his reluctant wife, hid the treasure in the Isle of Shoals chain. This is the story of a search for those gold and jewels and treasure, protected by the Ghost of White Island.

Title: The Third Day

- Author: Jeff Lovell
- Publisher: TotalRecall Publications, Inc.
- HARD COVER ISBN: 9781590959947
- PAPERBACK, ISBN: 9781590959954
- EBOOK, Nook, Kindle, ISBN: 9781590959961
- Number of pages: 288
- Publication Date: 2016

The Old, old man walks in all the countries of the world, tracing and retracing and tracing again his betrayal, unable to find peace or grace since his betrayal of the Nazarene some two thousand years ago. Two newlywed young people and their spouses find themselves called to help him and recover an incalculably valuable treasure, worth far more than any earthly price. The group must go to the Virgin Islands and recover the treasure to help the Old Man redeem his soul and save others from a disastrous fate at the hands of a desperate cult.

Title: Jazz and Ella

- Author: Jeff & Jacqi Lovell
- Publisher: TotalRecall Publications, Inc.
- PAPERBACK, ISBN: 9781590953006
- EBOOK, ISBN: 9781590953013
- Number of pages: 104
- Publication Date: 2015

Jazz and Ella tells the story of Jazz, a fourteen year old high school freshman, and his best friend, Ella, who meet on the way to Disney World. A supernatural being gives them each a magic amulet, which the children use to transport themselves to new and different worlds. They meet and deal many situations that cause them to face their fears and even terrors; that suggest ways that situations can be handled; and they see some of the choices that they will have to confront as they grow up.

Title: Gina and Colby

- Author: Jeff & Jacqi Lovell
- Publisher: TotalRecall Publications, Inc.
- PAPERBACK, ISBN: 9781590953259
- EBOOK, ISBN: 9781590953266
- Number of pages: 136
- Publication Date: 2016

A Magic Amulet Allows Two Teen-Agers to Discover how to Make a Difference in the World of Animal Poaching

Two teen-agers, different in every way, form an unshakeable friendship as a result of the adventures they share after meeting in Disney Springs. Transported through a magic amulet to a totally different culture and continent, they are offered an opportunity to make a difference in the lives of endangered animals.

Dangers abound as they face poachers and pirates in their attempts to rescue these creatures, and they discover a courage within themselves that leads each one to a positive change in how they view themselves and others.

Title: Marina and Dan

- Author: Jeff & JacqiLovell
- Publisher: TotalRecall Publications, Inc.
- HARD COVER ISBN: 978-1-59095-080-7
- PAPERBACK, ISBN: 978-1-59095-081-4
- EBOOK, Nook, Kindle, ISBN: 978-1-59095-082-1
- Number of pages: 128
- Publication Date: 2016

This ancient Egyptian Adventure, part of the Mousegate Series, traces the story of Marina and Dan, best friends since childhood, as they wrestle with the concept of heroism and how it applies to them. When offered a unique, but potentially dangerous opportunity by a spiritual being, they must make a decision that will stretch them in ways they never imagined. Able to experience first-hand the miraculous events that have been talked about for centuries, they witness the impossible become possible as they walk with Moses during the ancient biblical era where the crossing of the Red Sea took place. Both their friendship and their faith is strengthened through the adventures encountered together.

www.ingramcontent.com/pod-product-compliance
Lightning Source LLC
Chambersburg PA
CBHW020510120726
47904CB00003B/777